THE
LOVE LIST

A Comedy
by

Norm Foster

SAMUEL FRENCH, INC.
45 West 25th Street   7623 Sunset Boulevard
NEW YORK 10010   HOLLYWOOD 90046
LONDON   *TORONTO*

ISBN 0 573 63236 7   Printed in U.S.A.   #13818

IMPORTANT BILLING AND CREDIT REQUIREMENTS

THE LOVE LIST was first produced at the Thousand Islands Playhouse in Gananoque, Ontario, in October of 2003. The set and costumes were designed by Sue Lepage. The production was directed by Kelly Robinson with the following cast:

BILL...John Jarvis
LEON..C David Johnson
JUSTINE...Kristina Nicoll

CHARACTERS

Bill, *A statistician. 50.*

Leon, *A novelist. 50-55.*

Justine, *A mystery woman.*

TIME

The present. A Thursday.

PLACE

An apartment in the city. The apartment is an open concept place with the kitchen area Stage Right. and the living area Stage Left. There is either a kitchen table and chairs or an island with stools in the kitchen area, and a couple of chairs, a couch and a coffee table in the living room area. There is also a desk, a laptop computer, a phone and a CD player in the apartment. The apartment is overrun with books, magazines, newspapers and file folders.

ACT I

Scene 1

(As the lights come up, BILL and LEON ENTER the apartment. They have just come from a dinner to mark BILL's fiftieth birthday.)

LEON. Where in the hell do you find facts like that?

BILL. I'm a statistician. It's in my field of interest.

LEON. You mean to tell me that seventy percent of the dust in the home is comprised of human skin and hair?

BILL. That's right.

LEON. So, right now I'm standing here breathing in your dead skin and hair.

BILL. Not only mine. I've only lived here for seven years. You're also breathing in the dead skin and hair of the tenant before me and the one before that and who knows how far back. I mean, the person who lived here twenty years ago might be dead now, but if I swipe my finger across this table.. *(He runs his hand over the coffee table and then holds his finger up to LEON.)* There he is.

LEON. He's looking rather pale.

BILL. In fact, in the not too distant future, it might be possible to clone someone from their dust particles.

LEON. Is that why you're stockpiling it?

BILL. I've been busy. I haven't had a chance to houseclean.

Would you like a whiskey?

    LEON. Please.

(BILL goes to the kitchen and pours two glasses of whiskey.)

    LEON. So, what time should I pick you up tomorrow morning?

    BILL. Seven-thirty.

    LEON. Seven-thirty? Shit. And how long are you going to be gone?

    BILL. A week. The government's doing a housing survey up there and I have to oversee it.

    LEON. You're going to be back in time for the darts tournament I hope. I mean we are the Flaherty's Pub defending champions.

    BILL. I'll be back. Don't worry. Listen, thanks for buying me dinner tonight, Leon. That was very nice of you.

    LEON. Well, you only turn fifty once, Billy. I'm just sorry that Andrea couldn't join us but she's really under the weather. She sends her love though. Oh, and Peter says happy birthday too. He called home just before I left.

    BILL. How's he doing?

    LEON. Wonderfully well. Getting good marks. Captain of the volleyball team.

    BILL. Good for him. By the way, that book on globalization that I loaned him for his term paper? I'm going to need it for this urban living report I'm doing.

(BILL hands LEON a glass of whiskey.)

    LEON. I'll tell him. Well, here's to fifty years, my friend. *(He holds up his glass in a toast.)* And may you not spend one more without female companionship.

THE LOVE LIST

BILL. Don't start with this again.

LEON. I'm serious. The fact that a man has to be taken out on his fiftieth birthday by a friend, and a male friend no less, well, there is something deeply disturbing about that, Bill.

BILL. I'm fine.

LEON. No, you're not fine. Not yet. But, you soon will be.

BILL. What's that supposed to mean?

LEON. *(He hands BILL an envelope.)* Happy birthday.

BILL. What's this?

LEON. Open it.

BILL. You got me a present? Why are you spending your money on a present? The dinner was more than enough.

LEON. Oh, come now. I'm a successful novelist. I can afford to buy my best friend in the world a birthday present. Now open it.

BILL. Well, thank you. And you're not that successful.

LEON. It wasn't that expensive.

(BILL pulls a piece of paper out of the envelope and begins reading.)

BILL. The Love List. Ten qualities I am looking for in a mate.

LEON. What do you think?

BILL. What is it?

LEON. It's a mate finding service. I took the liberty of signing you up. It's called Got A Match.

BILL. Computer dating?

LEON. Oh, no. Not computers. That would be leaving too much to chance. No, these mates are found by an old Gypsy woman.

BILL. A what?

LEON. An old Gypsy woman. She owns the place. And she guarantees satisfaction.

BILL. You bought me a mate-finding service?

THE LOVE LIST

LEON. All you have to do is fill out the list, and take it back to her and she'll match you up with the woman of your dreams.

BILL. You can't be serious.

LEON. I'm dead serious. In fact, we'll fill it out right now and I'll take it back for you. Where's a pencil?

BILL. Leon, I am not going to look for a woman through a mate-finding service. I mean, God, why don't I just go out and get a hooker?

LEON. Let's wait and see if this pans out first.

BILL. Leon, forget it.

LEON. Billy, look, you have been divorced from Roxanne for seven years now and ever since then you've been having sex about as often as Albert Einstein did.

BILL. How do you know how often Albert Einstein had sex?

LEON. Oh, come on. You've seen pictures. Where the hell do you keep your pencils?

BILL. Leon, I am not going to do this. It's embarrassing.

LEON. Embarrassing?

BILL. Yes.

LEON. Do you want to know what's embarrassing? I'll tell you what's embarrassing, my friend. Sitting in a restaurant with a fifty year old man watching him blow out a candle on a goddamned cupcake while the staff gathers round and sings 'You're Sixteen, You're Beautiful, and You're Mine'. Now, fill out the form. *(Handing BILL a pencil.)* Besides, it's a birthday present. If you reject it you'll hurt my feelings. Is that what you want to do? Huh? Do you want to hurt the only friend you've got in this world?

BILL. All right, all right, I'll fill it out.

LEON. That's better.

BILL. But I am not going on a date with whoever this Gypsy finds for me.

LEON. Just fill out the form first. We'll worry about the rest

THE LOVE LIST

later.

BILL. Got A Match.

LEON. Never mind. It's a reputable company.

BILL. So, I have to write down the ten qualities that I am looking for in a woman.

LEON. That's right. In order of importance.

BILL. I don't know if I can come up with ten qualities.

LEON. Don't worry. I'll help you.

BILL. How do you know what I'm looking for?

LEON. Bill, I've known you for twenty-five years. Our desks were side by side at the newspaper for ten of those years. I know exactly what you're looking for. Besides, I'm a writer. I study the human condition. I can pull ten important qualities out of my head just like that.

BILL. All right. *(Looks at the list.)* Number one.

LEON. Oral sex.

BILL. What?

LEON. Oral sex.

BILL. Oral sex?

LEON. Very important. You want a woman who is comfortable in that arena.

BILL. That's number one?

LEON. Definitely.

BILL. Not strength of character perhaps? Kindness? Intelligence?

LEON. Bill, have you ever had incredibly good oral sex?

BILL. I didn't know it could be bad.

LEON. Just put it down.

BILL. No, I'm not putting that down. And especially not at number one. I'll just put down good lover. That's all encompassing.

LEON. No, no, no. Believe me, when it comes to sex you have to specify. You have to put down exactly what you want. You don't want any confusion on this point. Now, put it down.

BILL. All right, but I'm putting it at number ten.

LEON. Ten??

BILL. Ten.

LEON. You're putting nine things ahead of it?

BILL. .... All right, number four.

LEON. And you should probably write down, 'without having to ask for it'. It's so humiliating when you have to ask for it.

BILL. But, by writing it down, aren't I, in fact, asking for it?

LEON. Yes you are. Yes. But, this way you're asking for it in a lump sum right up front. You're not asking for it every time you want it.

BILL. Well, I think the two word description is more than enough. Now, what else do I look for in a woman?

LEON. She has to be gorgeous.

BILL. Oh, no. I am not writing down anything about appearance. That's superficial and demeaning.

LEON. You don't want an attractive woman?

BILL. I didn't say that. I would love an attractive woman, but look at me. What right do I have to ask for an attractive woman?

LEON. You don't think you're an attractive man?

BILL. No, I don't.

LEON. I think you're an attractive man.

BILL. You what?

LEON. I think you're very attractive.

BILL. You do?

LEON. Absolutely.

BILL. No, you're just saying that.

LEON. No, I mean it.

BILL. Cut it out.

LEON. Really.

BILL. Stop.

THE LOVE LIST

LEON. I can't believe you don't think you're attractive.

BILL. Well, I don't, so I am not asking for an attractive woman.

LEON. All right, fine. But, you don't want an unattractive one, right?

BILL. It doesn't matter to me one way or the other. A person's beauty is not found in their face anyway. It's found in their soul.

LEON. *(Begins to laugh.)* That's good. Soul.

BILL. Would you let me think please? I've got a nine-thirty flight tomorrow morning and I don't want to spend all night on this.

LEON. Fine. Think.

(LEON pours himself another drink.)

BILL. What about ambitious? I think there's something to be said for an ambitious woman. Someone who wants to be successful.

LEON. Most definitely. An ambitious woman would have a good career and there's nothing wrong with a woman with money.

BILL. All right. I'll put that at number...eight. *(He writes.)* Ah! And she should be well-versed in many subjects.

LEON. Why?

BILL. Well, because quite often I come home and I want to talk about the different surveys I'm working on, and about multivariate analysis or correlation coefficients...

LEON. I'm sorry. Did you say she should be well-versed or deceased?

BILL. For your information, Leon, the world of statistics is fascinating if you know what you're talking about. That's number three.

(He writes on the list.)

LEON. Oh! She trusts you. She's not jealous. Trust is very important in a relationship.

BILL. Yes, good. That's good. That'll be number... six. *(He writes.)* I'm surprised you thought of that one.

LEON. Why?

BILL. Well, with your history of infidelity.

LEON. I'll have you know I have not been unfaithful to Andrea in two years.

BILL. Two years? Congratulations. Don't you get a plaque for that?

LEON. You think it's easy? I can't tell you how many times, after one of my readings, that women come up to me and invite me back to their homes for coffee and cake. You think I don't know what coffee and cake is? I've had some of the nicest pieces of cake you can imagine.

BILL. Leon, it amazes me that Andrea has stayed with you as long as she has.

LEON. It's because Andrea is enlightened. She understands that as a writer, I have a need to experience life. To drink from an array of goblets.

BILL. That's a crock of shit.

LEON. It's not a crock of shit.

BILL. It's a crock of shit.

LEON. Bill, how can I be expected to write about women without having experienced a cross section of their gender first hand?

BILL. That's why it's called 'creative writing'. You're supposed to make it up.

LEON. Easy for you to say. Your life revolves around facts and figures. The only thing you have to be creative about is your filing system. God, look at this place. *(He picks up a magazine.)* How can you live like this?

BILL. Don't touch that!

LEON. Why?

BILL. Just put it back. I know where everything is.

THE LOVE LIST

LEON. In this mess?

BILL. Yes. If I need to look up something I know exactly where to find it.

LEON. Really?

BILL. I barely have to think about it.

LEON. All right, tell me this. How much time does the average person spend on the telephone in their life?

BILL. Two years.

LEON. But, how do you know that? Anybody can throw a number out there. I need proof.

BILL. In that stack of papers there, you'll find a Boston Herald third from the top.

(LEON moves to the stack and takes out the paper.)

Section E is the business section. Beneath the fold is an article on cell phones. There's a pie chart there.

LEON. *(Looks at the paper for a second.)* All right, so you know where everything is. I still say you need someone who can make this place presentable. Someone who's neat and tidy. Maybe you should write that down.

BILL. No. Nobody touches that material. The person that messes with that will feel the wrath of Bill. No, you know what I need? I need someone who won't try and change me. Someone who likes me just as I am. *(He writes.)* That's very good. That's number five.

LEON. All right, here's one. She speaks her mind. Tells you what she thinks. I mean the main problem that men have with women is that we never know what they're thinking, right?

BILL. Do we want to know?

LEON. *(Thinks for a second.)* Let's chance it.

BILL. *(He writes.)* That's number seven. God, I still need four more.

LEON. And you want a woman who will give you some quiet time when you ask her to. Andrea is extraordinary that way. When I'm working and she's tinkering around the house I find it very distracting, so all I have to do is tell her I need to be alone for a while and she leaves.

BILL. Just like that?

LEON. Just like that.

BILL. Where does she go?

LEON. ....I've never asked.

BILL. You've never asked?

LEON. No. I just assume that she goes shopping or visits friends.

BILL. That poor woman.

LEON. Just write it down. Someone who will leave when you ask them to.

BILL. No, that seems kind of submissive to me.

LEON. Not at all. It's thoughtful without being subservient. It shows that she cares.

BILL. All right. I'll put it at number nine. Oh, I've got it!

LEON. What?

BILL. She has to....No, on second thought, never mind.

LEON. What? What is it?

BILL. No, it's silly.

LEON. Is it something you want?

BILL. Yes. It's something I want very much.

LEON. Then what is it?

BILL. I..... I want her to enjoy kissing me.

LEON. You what?

BILL. I want her to enjoy it when we kiss. I always felt that Roxanne didn't like kissing me, and that hurt me. So I would want someone who likes to kiss me.

LEON. Put it down.

THE LOVE LIST

BILL. You think so?

LEON. Put it down. It's goddamned sensitive.

BILL. All right. *(He writes.)* That'll be number two. We just need two more.

LEON. Large breasts.

BILL. What?

LEON. Large breasts.

BILL. That's one of the important qualities you pull out of your head? Large breasts?

LEON. What's the matter with that?

BILL. God, for a novelist you are incredibly shallow, you know that?

LEON. William, there is nothing wrong with being shallow. Being shallow cuts through all of the crap. You don't have to explain why you like a painting. You can like it because it's the right size for your den. You don't understand Shakespeare, but you love a good western. You don't know what the hell Nietzsche was all about but you know what the Red Sox batted as a team against left-handers last year. No, I quite enjoy my shallowness. I wallow in shallow.

BILL. Oh, here's one. A sense of humour.

LEON. Oh, Bill, no.

BILL. What's the matter?

LEON. A sense of humour is such a clich?. It's mundane.

BILL. But, it's important.

LEON. No, believe me, a sense of humour is very overrated.

BILL. Oh, I see. A sense of humour is overrated, but gargantuan breasts are top ten material.

LEON. What can I say?

BILL. I'm putting it down.

(He writes.)

LEON. Not at number one I hope.

BILL. Number ten.

LEON. Fine. If it's number ten, I can live with it.

BILL. So, what happened in the last two years?

LEON. What about the last two years?

BILL. You said you've been faithful to Andrea for the last two years even though you've been offered coffee and cake. So why?

LEON. Ah, I don't know. I'm just...All right, I'm not getting as many cake offers as I used to. Maybe it's my age. I've got a kid in university for God's sake. I despise the fact that I'm that old. Or maybe it's my popularity. My last book was published two years ago and to tell you the truth, I don't get invited to do as many readings as I used to.

BILL. So, in other words, the opportunity for betrayal hasn't presented itself.

LEON. Sad, isn't it?

BILL. Terribly.

LEON. That reminds me. I've got to call my publisher. I sent him my new manuscript last week and this morning he leaves me a message saying he can't publish it.

BILL. He doesn't like it?

LEON. I don't care if he likes it or not. The man has no taste anyway.

BILL. He published your other books.

LEON. The point is, my contract calls for two more books and this is one of them. Now, come on. The list. One more.

BILL. No, you know what? This is pointless.

LEON. Pointless?

BILL. Yes. And besides, I've still got some figures to go over before I turn in.

(He opens a briefcase and takes out some work.)

THE LOVE LIST

LEON. Bill, one more. That's all we need. And it's the number one item.

BILL. No, I'm not going to follow up on this anyway.

LEON. All right, listen. Think back to your past.

BILL. Leon, it's almost midnight.

LEON. No, stay with me here. Think back to a woman who you were clear over the moon in love with. Can you think of anybody like that?

BILL. Sure I can. Why?

LEON. Who was it?

BILL. Her name was Justine.

LEON. Justine. Good. Tell me about her.

BILL. I met her in Ireland the summer after I finished university. She was from California and she was visiting relatives there and we had an intense two week relationship.

LEON. And what was it about this Justine that you liked so much?

BILL. Oh, God. Justine was... she was a spirit. I don't mean she had spirit. I mean she embodied it. When she walked it seemed like her feet didn't touch the ground, and her hair always had a breeze blowing through it. Even when there was no breeze. Even indoors, sitting in a pub, her hair had a breeze blowing through it. A warm ocean breeze. And being near her, you could feel the breeze yourself. You could smell it. You could taste the salt.

LEON. You surprise me sometimes, Bill.

BILL. Why?

LEON. That. What you just said. It was very lyrical. Enchanting. But, we can't put that shit down.

BILL. Why not?

LEON. Come on. Tastes like salt. Hair blowing. What the hell is that?

BILL. That's what she was like.

LEON. But what was the number one feature of her personality that made you crazy about her?

BILL. I think it was the fact that she was unpredictable. I never knew what she was going to do from one moment to the next.

LEON. No, we don't want to use that either.

BILL. Why?

LEON. Unpredictable? Why not just write down pre-menstrual?

BILL. But, I loved that about her. I was exactly the opposite. Everything about me was structured. It still is. But, Justine was spontaneous.

LEON. You like spontaneous?

BILL. Not in me, but in other people, yes. I mean, one minute she would be dancing down a cobblestone street, laughing and singing, and the next she would be steeped in thought about the plight of the homeless.

LEON. I believe the common term for that is schizophrenic.

BILL. I'm putting it down.

LEON. Bill, don't.

BILL. And it's number one.

LEON. Oh, God.

BILL. There we go. All finished. Can I get to work now?

(He hands the list to LEON.)

LEON. Hold on a second. Let's see what we've got here. *(He reads the list.)* Number ten; sense of humour. Number nine; leaves you alone when you ask her to. Number eight; ambitious. Number seven; speaks her mind. Number six; trusts you. Number five; won't try and change you. Number four; oral sex. Number three; well-versed in many topics. Number two; enjoys kissing you. And number one; unpredictable. I'm still fetched up on that last one. Unpredictable? She might kill you while you sleep.

BILL. Leon, that's it. That's my list. Take it or leave it.

LEON. All right, if you say so. I'll drop it off tomorrow. With any luck, you'll have your perfect match waiting for you when you get back.

BILL. No. Have you listened to anything I've said here?

LEON. Bits and pieces. Quite frankly Billy, a lot of what you say is humdrum.

BILL. Humdrum?

LEON. You're very pedestrian sometimes.

BILL. Why have we been friends all these years, Leon?

LEON. Because I'm lovable. You love me.

BILL. And what do you see in me?

LEON. You always keep a fine whiskey on hand.

BILL. You can go now.

LEON. Admit it, Billy. You love me.

BILL. Yes, I love you. Now, get the hell out.

LEON. By the way, what happened to Justine?

BILL. What?

LEON. You said you were madly in love with her. So, what happened?

BILL. She was killed in a car accident just after she returned to California.

LEON. Oh, God, that's a shame.

BILL. I'll never forget those two weeks in Ireland though. It was like we caught lightning in a bottle.

LEON. Well, let's hope this Gypsy can make some memories for you as well.

(Waving the list.)

BILL. No...

THE LOVE LIST

LEON. Happy birthday, dear friend.

(He EXITS.)

BILL. I am not following through with this!! I mean it, Leon! *(He closes the door.)* Got A Match.

(BILL goes back to his desk, sits down and spreads the work out in front of him. He uses the remote control to turn on the CD player. We hear music. He's feeling tired. He puts his head down on his desk. Lights down.)

Scene 2

(Time: About an hour later. Place: The same. The lights come up to reveal BILL, head down on the desk, fast asleep. His work is still spread out before him. We now hear a different song coming from the CD player. There is a knock on the door. The knocking awakens BILL.)

BILL. *(To himself.)* What? Oh. What time is it? *(There is another knock on the door. Bill turns off the CD player.)* Who is it?
JUSTINE. *(Off.)* It's Justine.
BILL. What? Who?
JUSTINE. *(Off.)* It's Justine, Bill. Open the door.
BILL. Justine? Justine who?
JUSTINE. That's not funny, Bill. Now, would you open the door please?

THE LOVE LIST

(BILL opens the door and JUSTINE ENTERS. She is dressed in business clothes and she carries a briefcase.)

JUSTINE. I'm sorry, honey. I left my key on the dresser this morning. Oh, God what a day. What a crazy day. I'm sorry I'm so late, baby. And especially on your birthday. Ooh, I'm sorry. *(JUSTINE gives BILL a kiss. BILL still stands there holding the door open. As JUSTINE talks, she sets her briefcase down, takes her jacket off and gets herself a drink.)* But, you know what happened? You're not going to believe this. That lanky son of a bitch Brian Mercer has been trying to steal the Willow Cosmetics account from me. That's why Mr. Jacobs wanted this meeting tonight. He was going to give Brian the account. So, I had to spend the whole evening kissing Mr. Jacobs' ass. It worked though. He gave me until Monday to lay out their new ad campaign. Can you believe that Brian Mercer? What the hell does he know about cosmetics? I wear the stuff every day. He only wears it on weekends.

BILL. Excuse me, but who are you?

(JUSTINE moves to the couch with her drink.)

JUSTINE. Oh, I'm sorry, baby. I know I'm not myself tonight, but that jerk Brian Mercer is really messing me up. Now, close the door and come over here.

BILL. I'm afraid not. Not until you tell me who...

JUSTINE. Uh-uh-uh-uh. *(She moves to BILL.)* No disagreements tonight, please? I've had a very disagreeable day.

(She closes the door.)

BILL. Now, hold on a second...

JUSTINE. No, no, no. Tonight, it's just you and me celebrating your birthday.

(She pulls BILL towards the couch and sits him down.)

BILL. How did you know it was my birthday?

JUSTINE. How did I know? You've been sleeping haven't you? You're groggy. Did you have too much wine with dinner?

BILL. Okay, wait a minute...

JUSTINE. How was it, by the way?

BILL. What?

JUSTINE. Your dinner with Leon and Andrea? You said they were taking you out?

BILL. When did I say that?

JUSTINE. Last night in bed.

BILL. In bed?

JUSTINE. You said that Leon and Andrea wanted to take us out for your birthday and I said I had this meeting and I didn't know how long it would last, so, you said you'd go with them and I said I'd try and catch up with the three of you later. So, how was it?

BILL. How was what?

JUSTINE. The dinner?

BILL. ...Andrea couldn't make it.

JUSTINE. What happened?

BILL. Nothing. She was...under the...not well.

JUSTINE. Nothing serious I hope.

BILL. No, she's just...you know, I'm feeling a little unnerved here.

(He breaks away from JUSTINE and stands near his desk.)

JUSTINE. About what?

THE LOVE LIST

BILL. About what? What do you think? You come in here. You make yourself at home. You tell me about a conversation we had that I don't remember.

JUSTINE. Well, I think your mind was on other matters.

(She moves to BILL.)

BILL. When?

JUSTINE. When we were in bed.

(She notices BILL's work on the desk.)

BILL. No, you see, that's the thing. I don't recall you and I ever....

JUSTINE. Oh, are these the urban living survey results?

BILL. Hmm? What?

JUSTINE. The urban living survey you did last week. Are these the results?

BILL. Yes. Yes, they are. How did you know about....

JUSTINE. Have you made the mean deviations and margin for error calculations yet?

BILL. Uh...yes I have, yes.

JUSTINE. Hmm-hmm. So, the majority feel that our cities are safer these days, do they?

(She sits.)

BILL. ...Well, that's just one of the findings.

JUSTINE. And is it true?

BILL. Hmm?

JUSTINE. Are they safer?

BILL. Well...actually crime stats are deceiving. *(He sits near*

JUSTINE.) For instance the murder rate is down not because fewer people are getting shot or stabbed, but because medical advances have improved a victim's chances for survival.

JUSTINE. Oh. And what were some of the other findings?

BILL. Other findings?

JUSTINE. Yes. Tell me what else you found out.

BILL. You want to talk about my survey?

JUSTINE. Oh, yes. And I want you to go into it deeply. But, don't rush. Take your time. Make it last.

BILL. All right. Uh...

JUSTINE. How big is the sample?

BILL. I'm sorry?

JUSTINE. The sample. How big is it?

BILL. Uh...twenty-five hundred returned out of eight thousand sent.

JUSTINE. Oh, that is big. That's more than double the minimum allowable.

BILL. Yes. Yes, it is.

(JUSTINE kisses BILL.)

JUSTINE. Oh,·God I like kissing you.

BILL. What?

JUSTINE. I said I like kissing you.

BILL. *(After a moment something dawns on him.)* Ahhhhh.

JUSTINE. What?

BILL. Ah-hah! Now I get it.

(He stands.)

JUSTINE. What?

BILL. Leon put you up to this!

THE LOVE LIST

JUSTINE. Up to what?

BILL. You know. The love list?

JUSTINE. Love list?

BILL. Yes, that was on it. She should enjoy kissing me.

JUSTINE. Who should enjoy kissing you?

BILL. You should.

JUSTINE. I've always enjoyed kissing you. What are you talking about?

BILL. *(Pointing to his work.)* And that was on it too. Well-versed. Oh, this is good.

JUSTINE. I don't understand.

BILL. Okay. Okay. Here's one for you. See if you can get this. What's a histogram?

JUSTINE. What?

BILL. A histogram. What is it?

JUSTINE. Bill, you know what a histogram is. Why are you asking me?

BILL. Yeah, I thought so. Well, you knew about the mean deviations. That's not bad. Good for you.

JUSTINE. A histogram is a way of graphically showing the characteristics of the distribution of items in a given population or sample.

BILL. ....That's right.

JUSTINE. Of course it's right.

BILL. But, how did you...I mean, you...

JUSTINE. All right, enough shop talk. Let's get down to business.

BILL. Business?

JUSTINE. Yes. Let's go to bed.

BILL. Bed?

JUSTINE. Yes.

BILL. You want to go to bed?

JUSTINE. Yes. I want to give you your birthday present.

BILL. My birthday present? Oh, business! Right! Number four!

JUSTINE. What?

BILL. Oh, this is very good. This is brilliant.

JUSTINE. *(Taking Bill's hand.)* Come on.

BILL. No, look, Justine—or whatever they call you—you don't have to do this.

JUSTINE. What do you mean, 'whatever they call me'? Whatever who calls me?

BILL. You know? On the street.

JUSTINE. On the street?

BILL. Yes. I mean you have been excellent. Magnificent. But the whole bed, birthday present thing, you should probably stop that.

JUSTINE. Why?

BILL. Well, it's bordering on teasing.

JUSTINE. I'm not teasing, Bill. You're going to be away for a week. Do you think I'm going to let you go away for a week without giving you something to remember me by? Now let's go.

BILL. Really?

JUSTINE. Yes, really.

BILL. You really want to go to bed?

JUSTINE. Yes:

BILL. With me?

JUSTINE. With you, yes. Now, follow me. And bring that big sample with you.

(She EXITS to the hallway, undoing her blouse.)

BILL. *(To himself.)* Well, Leon did say he'd be hurt if I rejected his birthday present. No, I'd better be a good friend and go to bed with this woman. *(He picks up some of his survey papers and EXITS to the hallway.)*

THE LOVE LIST

(Lights down.)

Scene 3

(Time: The next morning. Friday. Place: The same. As the scene opens there is a knock at the door. BILL ENTERS from the hallway carrying a suitcase. He sets the suitcase down, then goes to the door and opens it. LEON ENTERS feeling very tired. He carries a newspaper.)

LEON. Good morning. *(BILL hugs LEON.)* What was that for?

BILL. That was for last night.

LEON. It was just dinner. It wasn't that big a deal.

BILL. No, I don't mean the dinner. I mean the other thing.

LEON. The other thing? Oh, right. So, you liked that huh?

BILL. Oh, yes. I liked that very much. It was ingenious. Thank you.

LEON. You're welcome.

BILL. It's funny. I'm fifty years old, and I've never used that kind of service before. You know, paying money for it.

LEON. Well, there's a first time for everything. Do you have any orange juice?

BILL. Yes, help yourself. I was wondering. Do you think most men have gone that route at some point in their lives?

(LEON goes to the fridge and pours himself a glass of orange juice.)

LEON. It wouldn't surprise me.

BILL. You think so?

LEON. Sure. When I paid for yours there were three men and a woman in line ahead of me.

BILL. You're kidding??

LEON. No. I had to take a number and wait. It was like going to the deli.

BILL. My God. It's never crossed my mind to do that.

LEON. You've just got to be a little more amenable, Billy. The world is full of adventure if a man is receptive to new ideas.

(LEON begins to read the paper.)

BILL. Well, this one was inspired. You really outdid yourself.

LEON. Ah, it was nothing.

(JUSTINE ENTERS from the hallway.)

JUSTINE. Okay, I've got to run, Bill. Hi, Leon.

LEON. Hello.

JUSTINE. *(To BILL.)* Sorry I have to rush off, honey, but I've got to go home and change before I go to the office. You have a good flight, okay?

BILL. I will.

JUSTINE. Ooh, I'm going to miss you. *(JUSTINE gives Bill a kiss.)* I'm going to miss everything about you. Well, I'll miss some things more than others but we won't talk about that in mixed company.

BILL. There's that sense of humour I love so much.

JUSTINE. And there's that ass I love so much.

(She grabs BILL's behind.)

BILL. Oh, baby you're a wild one.

JUSTINE. And don't you forget it. *(She picks up her briefcase and moves to the door.)* Have a nice week. I'll be thinking about you.

BILL. Oh, I'll be thinking about you too. After last night, how could I think about anything else?

JUSTINE. I was good, wasn't I?

BILL. Were you ever. And so unpredictable.

JUSTINE. Okay, gotta run. Bye Leon.

(JUSTINE EXITS out the door.)

BILL. Okay, all set?

LEON. What the hell was that?

BILL. What?

LEON. That! The woman. What was she doing here?

BILL. She spent the night.

LEON. She what?

BILL. I was surprised too. I thought they usually engaged on an hourly basis but I guess I don't know too much about it.

LEON. About what?

BILL. Or maybe you paid her for the whole night. Is that what you did?

LEON. What the hell are you talking about? I've never seen that woman before in my life.

BILL. What?

LEON. Never.

BILL. Then how did she know your name?

LEON. I have no idea.

BILL. Yeah, right. You didn't buy her for me?

LEON. Buy her for you? No.

BILL. Oh, come on, Leon. You did so. She knew the qualities.

She did almost all of them.

LEON. What qualities?

BILL. The list we made up last night. The love list.

LEON. The love list? I've got that right here. *(He pulls the list out of his pocket.)* I was going to drop it off today.

BILL. Well, she knew them. Boy, did she ever know them. Now, let's go. I've got to get to the airport.

LEON. Bill, I'm telling you, I did not hire that woman for you.

BILL. Of course you didn't. And that's why she showed up at my door last night having been prepped on mean deviations and margin for error calculations, and that's why she said she likes kissing me. Now, come on. I'm going to be late.

LEON. When did she get here?

BILL. You know damn well when she got here. About an hour after you left which was just enough time for you to brief her on the list.

LEON. Bill, I swear, I am completely in the dark about this.

BILL. Leon, it's okay. I'm grateful to you. Hell, this is your one chance to look like a caring friend instead of a self-absorbed, unfeeling, adulterer.

LEON. I am not unfeeling.

BILL. Can we just go please?

(BILL opens the door then picks up his suitcase and briefcase.)

LEON. All right, but I didn't do this, Bill, and I won't say I did. I will not take credit for another man's handiwork. I'm a lot of things, but I am not a plagiarist. You must have some other friend out there who knows how inept you are in the romance department.

BILL. Hey, I am not inept. In fact, last night I was entirely ept. I was stunningly ept. And I believe Justine thought so too.

LEON. Who's Justine?

BILL. The woman. She said her name is Justine. Of course I'm sure it isn't. I'm sure that's something you told her to say.

LEON. I didn't tell her to say anything.

BILL. Then why did she insist on talking about my work? When we were in bed last night, even before we made love, we spent an hour talking about the central limit theorem.

(BILL EXITS out the door.)

LEON. Bill, my boy, you have got volumes to learn about foreplay.

(LEON EXITS out the door. Lights down.)

Scene 4

(Time: One week later. Place: The same. As the lights come up the door to the apartment opens and BILL ENTERS followed by LEON. BILL is carrying his suitcase and briefcase.)

BILL. Well, yeah, it was mostly work, but there was this one woman. Her name is Rachel. She was helping me out with the survey and we really hit it off. So anyway, she said she has business in town here next week, and she's going to give me a call when she gets here.

LEON. For a date?

BILL. No, no. Not a date. This is just two co-workers eating.

It's business.

LEON. So, what's she like?

BILL. She's very nice. She's shy. She's modest. She reminds me of one those southern belles you see in the movies. Very co-quettish. Oh, and she's really into statistics.

LEON. Gee, and she hasn't been snapped up yet?

BILL. Look, she might not be your kind of woman, Leon, but I like her. A lot.

LEON. But not enough to ask her out on a real date.

BILL. No, I'm not interested in dating. Why can't two people just go out, have dinner and enjoy each other's company?

LEON. Bill, that's what a date is.

BILL. No. A date could lead to a relationship and I don't want that. I'm no good at that. Just ask Roxanne. And how was your week?

LEON. My week? Well, it was pretty damned eventful actually.

BILL. Really? Why?

LEON. Remember I told you that sometimes when I'm work-ing, I ask Andrea to leave me alone for a while and she does?

BILL. Yeah.

LEON. And you asked me where she goes and I said I didn't know?

BILL. Uh-huh.

LEON. Well, I found out. She goes to her lover's apartment.

BILL. What?

LEON. That's right.

BILL. Andrea has a lover?

LEON. Andrea has a lover.

BILL. That's unbelievable.

LEON. Indeed.

BILL. Wow. How long has this been going on?

LEON. Seven years.

BILL. Seven years??

THE LOVE LIST

LEON. And all this time I thought she was being thoughtful by leaving me alone. Turns out my request for solitude was like a starter's pistol to her.

BILL. So, how did you find out?

LEON. Well, that's the strange thing, Bill. I asked.

BILL. You asked?

LEON. I asked. Two days ago she returned home after I had been working, and I innocently asked her where she had been. I thought I would show some interest as you suggested. Well, the question must have taken her by surprise because before you could say Bob's your uncle, she was spilling her guts about the entire affair. She said she had been dying to get it off her chest but didn't know how to approach the subject. She said my question was the opening she had been looking for, thank you very much.

BILL. So, who's the guy?

LEON. My publisher.

BILL. Oh, get out!

LEON. Without a word of a lie. Apparently he wasn't satisfied with just screwing me. And the night of your birthday, when Andrea told me she couldn't go to dinner with us because she was under the weather? She was under him.

BILL. On my birthday?

LEON. That's right.

BILL. Well, that's pretty damned inconsiderate. So, what are you going to do?

LEON. Oh God, Bill, I don't know. It's kind of late in the game to start looking for a new publisher.

BILL. I meant what are you and Andrea going to do.

LEON. Oh, well, we're finished. Andrea's moving out.

BILL. Oh, no.

LEON. She's home packing her things right now.

BILL. I'm sorry to hear that, Leon. How long have you two

been married now? Twenty-two years?

LEON. Twenty-three.

BILL. Twenty-three years. Boy, it's strange, isn't it? All this time you thought she was being understanding about your affairs because you were a writer, and here she was having an affair herself.

LEON. Actually, she said she went looking for the affair because of my affairs. She didn't expect it to last this long though. She thought that eventually I would ask where she had been spending her days, and she would tell me, thus making me jealous, and in some demented way, bringing us closer together.

BILL. But, you never asked.

LEON. Never did. So she just kept it up. I had no idea Andrea was that deceitful. It'll be a long time before a woman earns my trust again.

(JUSTINE ENTERS via the front door. She is carrying a bag of groceries and her briefcase.)

JUSTINE. Oh, you're home already. I was hoping to get here ahead of you and surprise you with dinner but I got tied up at the office. Hi, sweetie. *(She kisses BILL.)* Hi, Leon.

LEON. Hello.

JUSTINE. I guess the four-thirty flight was on time, was it? I'll get started on dinner right away. I hope you didn't eat too much on the plane. I know if I have that second bag of peanuts, I'm ready for a nap. Oh, God, I have to use the bathroom. *(She kisses BILL.)* It's so good to see you again. I'll be right back.

(JUSTINE EXITS into the hallway.)

LEON. What in the name of Julie Andrews is going on here?

THE LOVE LIST

BILL. You tell me, Leon.

LEON. What?· No, I've got nothing to do with this. I do not know that woman.

BILL. Well, what's she doing here? How did she know what flight I was on?

LEON. I haven't a clue.

BILL. Well, I didn't tell anybody but you because you were the one who was picking me up.

LEON. Bill, I swear to you, I have no idea. I'm as gobsmacked as you are.

BILL. So, you didn't hire her?

LEON. Listen, I'm putting a kid through university and now I'm looking at a divorce settlement. I cannot afford to be underwriting your love life.

BILL. Well, what am I supposed to do about this?

LEON. Well, the first thing I'd do is find out who did hire her, and how long you've got her for. If it's only for an hour, you might want to forego the dinner.

BILL. Leon, I'm serious.

LEON. So am I. If somebody put down some hard earned money for this woman, who are you to play fast and loose with it?

BILL. How much would something like this cost?

LEON. Five hundred dollars. It's a guess.

BILL. But, I can't think of anybody who would do a thing like this outside of you. Come on, Leon, it's you, isn't it? I know it is.

LEON. No.

BILL. Come on. Admit it.

LEON. It's not me! Hell, maybe nobody paid for her. Maybe she's here on her own. Did you ever think of that?

BILL. But for what purpose? What does she want?

LEON. She wants you obviously.

BILL. But why? Why me? You don't think she's stalking me,

do you? Maybe she's a stalker and she's got this fixation about me.

LEON. Oh yeah, I think fifty year-old civil servants are high on a lot of stalkers' lists. In fact, I believe it goes; movie stars, rock stars, middle aged civil servants who nobody GIVES A SHIT ABOUT!!

(JUSTINE ENTERS. She moves to the kitchen and begins putting groceries away and preparing dinner.)

JUSTINE. I wasn't sure what to make you tonight so I bought a little bit of everything. Portobello mushrooms, romaine lettuce, chicken breasts, strawberries. Do you want to stay for supper, Leon?

LEON. Oh, no, that's fine.

JUSTINE. Are you sure? We've got plenty.

LEON. No, you kids haven't seen each other in a week. I'm sure you'd rather be alone, so, I'll get going.

BILL. What, right now?

LEON. Yeah.

BILL. You're leaving right now? This minute?

LEON. I'm having drinks with my lawyer at six. Besides, I wouldn't want to overstay my welcome. I hate people who mill about when they're not wanted? Don't you, Justine?

JUSTINE. With a passion.

LEON. I'll bet with a passion. All right. I'm off.

BILL. Leon...

LEON. Oh, listen don't forget about the darts tournament to-morrow night.

BILL. The what?

LEON. The darts tournament.

BILL. Oh, dammit. Look, I don't know if I can make that, Leon.

LEON. What?

BILL. Well, I've got to analyze the results of the housing survey and prepare the findings. And I've still got to finish that urban living report.

JUSTINE. Oh, go, Bill.

BILL. What?

JUSTINE. Go. Have some fun. You don't get out enough. Your work can wait one day, can't it?

LEON. Boy, don't let this one get away, Billy.

JUSTINE. And you two are the defending champions. They'll be expecting you.

BILL. Uh..well, I suppose I could put the reports off for one more day.

LEON. Then it's settled. I'll see you tomorrow. Goodbye Justine.

JUSTINE. Bye, Leon. Give my love to Andrea.

LEON. Andrea? Right. I'll do that.

(LEON EXITS.)

JUSTINE. Why is he meeting with his lawyer?

BILL. Hmm?

JUSTINE. He said he was meeting his lawyer for drinks. Is there a problem?

BILL. Oh, it's just...Can I ask you something?

JUSTINE. Sure, babe. What is it?

BILL. Why exactly are you here?

JUSTINE. Well, I knew you wouldn't feel like cooking after your flight so I thought I'd do it for you.

BILL. No, I mean was this Leon's idea or somebody else's or what?

JUSTINE. It was my idea. Plus, I haven't seen you in a week and I missed you.

BILL. Uh-huh. Let me ask you something else. How did you know that Leon and I are the defending champions?

JUSTINE. Well, you only won it a month ago. My memory's not that bad.

BILL. Okay, this has been fascinating to say the least, and I don't know how you've done it but it is quite an accomplishment and you are to be commended. Unfortunately, it's starting to frighten me so here's the plan.

JUSTINE. Wait a minute, wait. Let me tell you my plan first.

BILL. No, please, just hear me out..

JUSTINE. No, really Bill, I think you'll like my plan. Here it is. Listen. Now, I know you're tired from your trip, so why don't you relax for a bit while I make supper, then after supper we'll slip into the tub and let our worries and cares drop away like a pair of satin panties. Then once our minds are free of troublesome thoughts, we'll go to bed and fill them up with sensuous ones.

BILL. .....That's a good plan too.

JUSTINE. Now you just sit back and take it easy. Tell me about your week. How was it?

BILL. My week?

JUSTINE. Yes. Was it busy? Boring? What?

BILL. Oh, I see. We're going to chat like couples do at the end of a long day.

JUSTINE. We most certainly are. I've missed our end of day chats this week.

BILL. That's cute. Well, my week was pretty hectic. We only had five days to conduct the survey and three of the staffers were off with the flu so two of us had to do the entire job.

JUSTINE. Oh, no. That must have been awful.

BILL. Well, it was frantic there for a while.

JUSTINE. I can imagine. *(Beat.)* Aren't you going to ask me about mine?

BILL. Your what?

JUSTINE. My week, silly.

BILL. Oh right. My turn. Okay. How was your week?

JUSTINE. You don't want to know.

BILL. No, I do. I really do. Did you present your ad campaign to your boss?

JUSTINE. Yes I did.

BILL. And?

JUSTINE. He liked it. He liked it very much.

BILL. Good.

JUSTINE. But he gave the account to Brian Mercer anyway because he said Brian has a better sense of the client's needs. Do you believe that?

BILL. Bastard.

JUSTINE. What really annoys me is that Brian's campaign is all wrong for Willow Cosmetics. They're a very classy outfit and he's got them pitching their product like some third-rate used car salesmen.

BILL. Willow Cosmetics. I don't think I've heard of them.

JUSTINE. Bill, they're only the second largest cosmetics manufacturer in the country.

BILL. They are?

JUSTINE. Yes.

BILL. Well, don't you worry. Brian Mercer isn't half the ad person you are. And before long people are going to realize that.

JUSTINE. It's nice of you to say that, sweetie, but sometimes I get discouraged that's all.

BILL. Well, don't. You just stick with it.

JUSTINE. Oh I plan to. This is just a temporary setback. Brian's going to find out that I am not the kind of person you want to stab in the back.

BILL. That's the spirit.

JUSTINE. Before I'm done, I'll be running that agency. You mark my words.

BILL. Ah. Ambition. Very good. You know, I think I'm starting to get the hang of this. What the hell? I'm going to open a bottle of wine. We'll drown your sorrows together.

(He opens a bottle of wine.)

JUSTINE. I knew I could count on you to cheer me up. You're always there when I need you, Bill.

(She gives BILL a kiss.)

BILL. Mmm. That's a nice touch.

JUSTINE. What is?

BILL. Salt. You taste like salt. What did you do, rub some on your lips?

JUSTINE. Of course not. Why would I do that?

BILL. So you could.....it's not important.

JUSTINE. We should have Leon and Andrea over sometime soon. I haven't seen Andrea in ages.

BILL. Actually, Leon and Andrea are splitting up.

JUSTINE. What?

BILL. I'm afraid so. Leon told me just before you came in.

JUSTINE. Did Andrea finally get sick of him screwing around on her?

BILL. God, you do know everything, don't you? Well, as it turns out, she was screwing around on him too.

JUSTINE. You're kidding.

BILL. No, really. For the last seven years.

JUSTINE. Well, I'll be damned. It's always the mousy ones isn't it? Who would have known? Sweet little Andrea wouldn't say sex if she had a mouthful of it. Next thing you know she's standing on the pier waving in the sailors.

THE LOVE LIST

BILL. You know something?
JUSTINE. What?
BILL. I'm starting to like this.

(They toast and drink. Lights down.)

Scene 5

(Time: The next morning. Place: The same. As the lights come up BILL ENTERS from the bedroom. He's singing to himself. He could be singing along to a song on his CD player. He moves to the counter and pours himself a cup of coffee. He then moves to his computer to work and turns off the music. After a moment, JUSTINE ENTERS. She is in her nightclothes.)

JUSTINE. Morning, honey.
BILL. Good morning.
JUSTINE. What time is it?
BILL. Almost eleven.
JUSTINE. Really? Oh. I slept in. Sorry.
BILL. That's all right. I've been working on these survey results.
JUSTINE. On a Saturday?
BILL. I wanted to get a jump on them.
JUSTINE. You work too hard, Bill. You really do. But, I'm not going to try and change you. No. I like you just fine the way you are.
BILL. Number five.

JUSTINE. What?

BILL. Number five on the love list. Won't try and change me.

JUSTINE. What is this love list you keep..oh, is that coffee?

BILL. Yeah. It's on the counter.

JUSTINE. Oh, good.

(She moves to the stove to pour herself a coffee.)

BILL. You know I had a terrific time last night.

JUSTINE. Yeah, me too. It was nice.

BILL. In fact, I can't remember when I've had such an all around satisfying night.

JUSTINE. I'm glad.

BILL. And do you know what I really enjoyed?

JUSTINE. What?

BILL. Just lying in bed and talking to you.

JUSTINE. Well, I hope that's not all you enjoyed.

BILL. Oh, no. Certainly not.

JUSTINE. Good. Because I hate it when men use me for my brain. I'm more than that. I'm a sexpot too dammit. Speaking of which, the next time we make love, Bill, could you try and hang on a little longer?

BILL. ...Pardon me?

JUSTINE. When we make love. I'd like it to last a little longer. That way it would be a teensy bit more satisfying for yours truly. And I think it would be nice if I got just as much pleasure out of it as you do.

BILL. Oh.

JUSTINE. And some foreplay might help too. Take your time with me. Search out the points on my body that are the most sensitive. Or would you rather I just told you where they are?

BILL. No, no. I'll look for them.

THE LOVE LIST

JUSTINE. I hope you don't mind my being right up front about this.

BILL. No.

JUSTINE. Because if I don't tell you what I want, how will you know?

BILL. Right. Number seven. Speaks her mind.

JUSTINE. What?

BILL. It wasn't bad was it? I mean, I hope it wasn't unpleasant for you.

JUSTINE. What, the sex?

BILL. Yes.

JUSTINE. Oh, no. No, it wasn't bad at all.

BILL. Good. I'm encouraged.

JUSTINE. So, what are your plans today? Do you feel like going out for some breakfast?

BILL. I'd love to but I've already eaten.

JUSTINE. Oh.

BILL. And I'm on a bit of a roll here with the work so I don't want to stop. But, if you want to go and eat, you go right ahead.

JUSTINE. No, it wouldn't be the same without you. Maybe I'll just make this a pajama day.

BILL. Really?

JUSTINE. Uh-huh.

BILL. You're staying around?

JUSTINE. Yes. Is that all right?

BILL. Certainly. Of course. I just thought that once the night was over, you'd be leaving.

JUSTINE. Oh, no. I've got no place to be today.

BILL. You're not going back to..uh..you know, work?

JUSTINE. Oh, God no. I'm going to try and put work and Brian Mercer right out of my mind today. I should do these dishes though.

BILL. No, listen, you don't have to do that. I'll clean those up later.

JUSTINE. *(Moving to the dishes. She puts on a pair of rubber gloves.)* No, I don't mind. I mean, you know me and my obsession with tidiness.

BILL. Your what?

JUSTINE. My obsession with tidiness.

BILL. Tidiness? That wasn't on the list.

JUSTINE. What?

BILL. Nothing. Are you sure you want to tackle those dishes?

JUSTINE. Positive. You just go ahead and work.

BILL. Okay. *(JUSTINE begins clanging around in the kitchen area and BILL goes back to his work. After a few seconds, the noise begins to get to BILL.)* Actually, Justine?

JUSTINE. Yes?

BILL. I wonder if I could ask you a favour.

JUSTINE. Sure, sweetie. What is it?

BILL. Well, when I'm working on something like this, I really need to be focused.

JUSTINE. Sure.

BILL. And, well, I find external noises very distracting. So, I wonder if it would be too much to ask if you could uh...

JUSTINE. If I could what?

BILL. Well, if you could leave me alone for a while.

JUSTINE. Okay.

(JUSTINE stops doing the dishes and moves towards the door.)

BILL. I mean if you want to come back when I'm done that would be fine. I'm not sure how long it will be but... *(JUSTINE EXITS out the door, still wearing the rubber gloves. To himself.)* ....Well, that was easy enough. *(BILL goes back to his work. After a couple of seconds there is a knock on the door.)* Come in! *(The door opens. LEON ENTERS. BILL doesn't see him.)* You're feeling underdressed I'll bet.

LEON. *(Looking at his clothing.)* Not particularly.

(BILL turns to LEON.)

BILL. Leon. I thought you were someone else.

LEON. Uh-huh. Listen, I'm heading over to Flaherty's for their steak and eggs breakfast. I've decided to kill myself with an overdose of cholesterol. You wanna watch?

BILL. No thanks. I had breakfast three hours ago.

LEON. All right, so I'm running behind today. It's my first official day of bachelorhood and I'm at loose ends.

BILL. Andrea's gone, is she?

LEON. She left last night.

BILL. Where'd she go?

LEON. I didn't ask. I've learned my lesson. And what about your friend?

BILL. Hmm?

LEON. Justine. Is she still here?

BILL. What do you mean? She just walked out the door. Didn't you see her?

LEON. See her where?

BILL. Out in the hall. The woman in her nightclothes.

LEON. I didn't see any woman in her nightclothes.

BILL. Leon, she left three seconds before you knocked. You must have seen her.

LEON. No, I didn't see anybody.

BILL. Oh, come on.

LEON. I'm serious. She wasn't out there.

BILL. You're putting me on, right?

LEON. Bill, don't start with this again. I have had it with you and your mystery woman. Now, come to breakfast with me.

BILL. No, I've got work to do.

LEON. Forget the work. You've got a friend who needs consoling. That's far more important.

BILL. You need consoling? I find that hard to believe.

LEON. Why?

BILL. Leon, it's you we're talking about here.

LEON. You must think that I am completely insensitive. Is that what you think?

BILL. Yes.

LEON. Bill, my wife just walked out on me. The woman I shared my life with for twenty-four years.

BILL. I thought it was twenty-three.

LEON. She told me last night it was twenty-four. One must have been a leap year. Besides, I had a meeting with my lawyer last night and he says if my libidinous publisher won't publish my new book, there's nothing we can do about it. So, I've got that preying on my mind as well. Now, come. Have breakfast with me. Please.

BILL. Oh, all right. I suppose I can go for an hour.

LEON. Thank you.

BILL. But, no more than an hour.

LEON. Fine. We shall console with haste.

BILL. Just let me get washed up first.

(BILL EXITS to the hallway. LEON sits and takes the love list out of his pocket.)

LEON. So, Bill, with everything that happened with Andrea this week, I forgot to turn in your love list to the Gypsy woman at Got A Match.

BILL. *(Off.)* Well, don't bother.

LEON. You don't want it now?

THE LOVE LIST

BILL. *(Off.)* No thanks.

LEON. Yes, I figured that, what with Justine being here and all. So as long as it's already paid for I thought I might use it myself. It might help me through the pain of the breakup. Would that be all right?

BILL. *(Off.)* Be my guest.

LEON. And I changed one of the qualities here to suit me a little more. I mean I'm only slightly more adept than you at keeping a clean domicile so I changed unpredictable to tidy.

(BILL ENTERS with a towel.)

BILL. You changed what?
LEON. Unpredictable to tidy.
BILL. When did you do that?
LEON. This morning.

(JUSTINE ENTERS through the front door.)

JUSTINE. I'm back. Hi, Leon.
LEON. Hello.
BILL. Justine, did you forget something?
JUSTINE. No. Why?
BILL. Well, your, uh...

(Pointing to her clothes.)

JUSTINE. You said I could come back when you're finished.
BILL. No, that's not what I meant.
JUSTINE. You are finished, right?
BILL. Yes, I am. How did you know?
JUSTINE. A woman just knows these things.

(She moves to the dishes.)

BILL. Uh-huh. Well, Leon and I are heading out, so you can make as much noise as you like now.

(He starts for the bedroom.)

JUSTINE. You're going out?

BILL. *(Stopping.)* Just for an hour. We're going for breakfast.

JUSTINE. Oh. I see.

BILL. Why? What's wrong?

JUSTINE. Nothing. It's just that when I asked you to go out, you said you'd already eaten breakfast.

BILL. Well, yes, but Leon didn't want to eat alone this morning.

JUSTINE. Oh.

BILL. You know, because of Andrea and all.

JUSTINE. Right. I'm sorry to hear about Andrea, Leon.

LEON. Thank you.

JUSTINE. *(To Leon.)* It's funny you know because I told Bill that I didn't feel like eating breakfast alone, but he had all of this work to do.

BILL. This isn't the same, Justine. I mean, Leon's feeling down.

JUSTINE. Oh, I know.

BILL. And I'm just going along to cheer him up.

JUSTINE. Absolutely. And I think that's exactly what a good friend should do.

BILL. Good. So, I'll just go and finish getting ready.

(He starts for the bedroom but stops again when JUSTINE speaks.)

JUSTINE. Yes. And let's be thankful that you turned down my breakfast invitation. Otherwise we would have been gone when Leon got here and he would have had to eat alone. Whatever would you have done, Leon?

LEON. I have no idea.

JUSTINE. Well, you won't have to find out, will you?

LEON. No, I suppose I won't. Come on, Bill let's go.

BILL. I'll be right out.

LEON. No, Bill, let's go now.

BILL. What?

LEON. You can wash up at the pub.

BILL. I'll be one second.

(BILL ENTERS to the hallway. There is an awkward pause.)

LEON. Chilly out.

JUSTINE. Is it?

LEON. You mean you didn't notice?

JUSTINE. No, I didn't.

LEON. Oh. *(There is another awkward pause.)* Did you know that seventy percent of the dust in the home is comprised of..

JUSTINE. Human skin and hair, yes.

LEON. Oh, you knew.

JUSTINE. Uh-huh.

LEON. They might be able to clone people out of dust bunnies one day.

JUSTINE. You don't have to avoid talking about it, Leon.

LEON. About what?

JUSTINE. You and Andrea.

LEON. Oh, of course.

JUSTINE. You're not upset that Bill told me are you?

LEON. No. Just a bit surprised, that's all.

JUSTINE. You shouldn't be. Bill and I don't have any secrets. If you tell him something, you tell me too.

LEON. Well, consider me alerted then.

JUSTINE. You love her very much, don't you? *(Leon doesn't answer.)* It's all right. You don't have to say it. It's in your face. In your eyes. In the way you stand. It's in everything you do. And now it's over. What a shame. After twenty-four years. Well, that will never happen with Bill and I.

LEON. Bill and you?

JUSTINE. Yes, because we have a relationship built on trust. I trust him and he trusts me. We both know that the other one wouldn't dream of being unfaithful.

LEON. A relationship?

JUSTINE. Built on trust, yes.

LEON. Uh-huh. Well, you know Justine, Andrea and I are a lot different than you and Bill.

JUSTINE. Oh, I know.

LEON. And our relationship was a lot different.

JUSTINE. You can say that again.

LEON. Yes. For one thing, we had one.

JUSTINE. What's that supposed to mean?

LEON. A relationship. We had one. We were married.

JUSTINE. Just because Bill and I aren't married, doesn't mean a serious commitment hasn't developed over time.

LEON. Justine, in the length of time you two have been together, prickly heat couldn't develop.

(BILL ENTERS from the hallway.)

BILL. I'm all set. *(To JUSTINE.)* Justine, are you going to stay around or...

JUSTINE. Yes, I still have those dishes to do. But first I think

THE LOVE LIST

53

I'll soak in the tub and read for a while. I brought a book of Tennyson with me.

BILL. All right, but, you know when I get back I'm going to have to work.

JUSTINE. Oh, I know. Don't worry. I'll make myself scarce if you want me to. *(She gives BILL a kiss.)* Bye sweetie.

BILL. Bye.

JUSTINE. Goodbye, Leon.

LEON. Goodbye.

(JUSTINE EXITS to the hallway.)

BILL. Tennyson. That's her favourite poet.

LEON. Boy, how screwed up do you have to be to have a favourite poet?

BILL. No, she's amazing. She really is. She's everything I like in a woman. I mean we had such a great time in bed last night.

LEON. No, stop right there. Please. Do I need to hear this?

BILL. I don't mean the sex. I mean, before that. Talking about surveys, and ad campaigns, and Tennyson.

LEON. I'm surprised you managed to stay awake for the sex.

(JUSTINE ENTERS from the hallway.)

JUSTINE. I forgot my book. Oh, by the way, Leon, I meant to tell you, I finally got around to reading your novel 'Beyond Twilight' last night.

LEON. You read it in one night?

JUSTINE. It's not a difficult read.

(She takes a book out of her briefcase.)

LEON. I see. And what did you think?

JUSTINE. Well, it was a bit pedantic at times.

LEON. Pedantic?

JUSTINE. Yes. And the resolution wasn't entirely satisfying, but overall I thought it was a very promising first effort.

LEON. It's my fifth book.

JUSTINE. Oops. Well, in that case I would have to say it was a slightly substandard offering.

LEON. Is that a fact?

JUSTINE. I hope you don't mind my saying so.

LEON. No, not at all.

BILL. She likes to speak her mind.

LEON. Yes, isn't that precious?

JUSTINE. Well, my bath awaits. Bye-bye.

(JUSTINE EXITS to the hallway.)

BILL. Isn't she extraordinary, Leon? She makes me feel like a kid again. Like when you had a crush on a girl in school and it was a thrill just to hear her say your name. Remember how it used to give you butterflies in your stomach? Well, that's what she does. She gives me butterflies.

LEON. Yes, I'm feeling a little something down there myself.

BILL. And you know what else?

LEON. What?

BILL. She likes to kiss me.

LEON. Uh-huh.

BILL. No, she really does. She kisses me all the time. And her lips are so soft, like strawberry jelly.

LEON. All right, thank you. You can stop with the lips.

BILL. And when I was working, and I asked her to leave, she left that instant. No questions asked. It was like you said. Thoughtful without being subservient. I'm telling you, Leon, she is unbelievable.

LEON. Bill, aren't you overlooking a very salient point here?

BILL. What point?

LEON. Who the hell is she? Where did she come from?

BILL. I don't care about that anymore.

LEON. Don't care about it?

BILL. No. Let's go.

LEON. Wait a minute. What do you mean you don't care?

BILL. I don't. I was thinking about that this morning. I'm fifty years old, I'm not that attractive, and I'm dull.

LEON. What? You're not dull.

BILL. I am. You said so yourself. I'm humdrum. Pedestrian. I'm so dull, my wife left me out of sheer boredom. Yeah, you didn't know that. I was too embarrassed to tell you. She said she wanted a divorce because I bored the hell out of her. And then along comes this woman—from wherever—and for some reason, she seems to like me. And she's smart and she's sexy and she likes me. And she kisses me, and she talks to me in bed and she listens to me as if what I have to say is important to her. As if it means something. And she kisses me, Leon. I can't question all of that. I'm afraid if I do, it'll end.

LEON. And what if she's being paid to do all those things?

BILL. By who? No, I don't think she is. I mean, why would she stay around when I'm not even going to be here? No, I don't know where she came from, or when she's going to leave again, but I've decided that I'm going to enjoy her for as long as I can.

LEON. I don't like it, Bill.

BILL. Well, maybe you're jealous.

LEON. Jealous? I'm not jealous.

BILL. No, I think maybe you are. I think you see me with this terrific woman and your wife has left you and you're not getting those cake invitations anymore and I think you're jealous.

LEON. All right, look, I'm not going to argue with you about this. I just know that something is terribly, terribly wrong here.

BILL. You're right. Something is wrong, Leon. I should be going to breakfast with Justine.

LEON. What? ·

BILL. I think she was hurt that I was going to breakfast with you. No, I've got a better idea. I'll make her breakfast. She deserves that.

(BILL moves to the kitchen area.)

LEON. Bill?

BILL. I'm sorry, Leon. You're going to have to go to breakfast yourself.

LEON. Oh, for God's sake. Are you serious?

BILL. I've never been more serious. Now, let's see. What would she like?

LEON. Bill, listen to me.

BILL. No, Leon. Whatever you have to say will have negative connotations and I don't want to hear it.

(He takes a frying pan out of the cupboard.)

LEON. You're really hooked on this woman, aren't you?

BILL. Yes. I think I'm being swept off my feet by her.

LEON. Fine. Get swept. But, when the truth is finally revealed about this person, don't say I didn't warn you. *(He moves towards the door.)* I'll see you at the darts tournament tonight. Or will you still be playing spank the cook with Justine?

BILL. Don't worry. I'll be there. *(To himself.)* Maybe poached eggs. No! Eggs Benedict. Yes. Eggs Benedict and cinnamon pota-

toes. *(LEON EXITS. BILL calls down the hall to JUSTINE.)* Justine?!
This morning I belong to you, darling!

(Lights down. End Act One.)

THE LOVE LIST

ACT II

Scene 1

(Time: Later that night. Place: The same. As the scene opens there is no one onstage. The books, magazines and newspapers are gone. The apartment is spotless. BILL and LEON ENTER through the front door.)

LEON. I still say you were distracted.

BILL. I was not distracted.

LEON. You were playing as if you were distracted. You didn't make a shot all night.

BILL. Well, you didn't do much better you know.

LEON. At least I didn't put a dart into the wall clock.

BILL. I hit the twelve, didn't I?

LEON. I was embarrassed, Bill. You had patrons diving for cover all night.

(BILL notices the missing magazines and newspapers.)

BILL. Ah!!! What happened here??

LEON. Holy shit. Will you look at that?

BILL. My magazines. My newspapers. My research.

LEON. It certainly opens the place up.

BILL. Oh my God!

(JUSTINE ENTERS from the hallway. She has been cleaning. She's wearing rubber gloves.)

JUSTINE. Bill, you're home already? It's barely midnight. Hello, Leon.

LEON. Hello.

JUSTINE. So, how was it tonight?

BILL. Justine?

JUSTINE. Yes?

BILL. What happened here?

JUSTINE. Do you like it?

BILL. Do I like it? Where is everything?

JUSTINE. I moved it all into the spare room. It's much tidier, don't you think?

BILL. But, that's my research material.

JUSTINE. Well, it's still here. It's just in the other room.

BILL. But, is it in the same order?

JUSTINE. Order? What order?

LEON. Could I pour myself a drink? I wasn't going to stay but maybe just the one.

(LEON pours himself a drink.)

BILL. They were in order, Justine. All the magazines, the newspapers, the files. I knew where everything was.

JUSTINE. Oh.

BILL. So, did you keep them in the same order?

JUSTINE. Well, no I just stacked them up willy nilly.

BILL. Willy nilly?

JUSTINE. Did I do something wrong?

THE LOVE LIST

BILL. Well, it's just that...I mean...

JUSTINE. It's just what?

LEON. Yes, go ahead, Bill. It's just what?

JUSTINE. Oh, I hope I didn't do anything wrong. I thought I was helping you. You're so busy all the time, I just thought you didn't have time to tidy it up yourself.

BILL. Well, I...

JUSTINE. Are you mad at me?

BILL. Well...

JUSTINE. Because if you are, I can put it all back. Would you like me to? What would you like me to do, Bill?

LEON. Yes, Bill, what would you like her to do?

BILL. ....Well, I guess it does look tidier.

LEON. What?

JUSTINE. Yes, I thought so too. It's much less cluttered.

BILL. And it was a bit of a fire hazard too I suppose.

JUSTINE. Oh, it was definitely a fire hazard. So, you like it?

BILL. Well...yes, I guess I do.

LEON. Oh, God.

JUSTINE. What's the matter, Leon?

LEON. Hmm? Oh. Whiskey's off. No bite to it. No guts.

JUSTINE. So, how did it go tonight? Did you win?

BILL. No. We finished eighth.

LEON. Out of eight teams.

JUSTINE. Oh, that's too bad. What happened?

LEON. Well, Bill here seemed to be distracted.

BILL. I wasn't distracted.

LEON. Well, you played as if you were distracted.

JUSTINE. Distracted by what?

LEON. By the scorekeeper.

BILL. I was not distracted by the scorekeeper.

JUSTINE. Why? What was the scorekeeper doing?

LEON. She was being voluptuous. And at one point, she inadvertently spilled a beer down her front, and apparently her beer was much colder than the ones the rest of us were consuming. It was at this point that young William here took dart in hand and skewered the establishment's wall clock.

JUSTINE. Well, that doesn't sound like Bill. Bill doesn't lust after women like that.

BILL. Thank you, Justine.

LEON. I didn't say he was lusting after her. I said he was distracted by her. I was lusting after her, but at least I managed to keep my concentration. And how do you know what Bill does or doesn't do?

JUSTINE. Well, I think I know Bill better than anybody. Right, sweetie?

BILL. Well, you seem to know me pretty damned well, I'll say that.

JUSTINE. Oh, I know you like the back of my hand.

LEON. Really? Then why didn't you know that he wouldn't want you messing about with his research material?

JUSTINE. Well, that's not a big issue, is it, Bill?

BILL. No. No, it's minor. A small transgression.

LEON. A small transgression? What happened to the wrath of Bill?

BILL. Leon, it'll take me a day to put it back in order. It's nothing.

LEON. No, it's nothing now, but when I touched it I was dead man walkin'.

JUSTINE. I think Leon's just upset about losing his darts championship.

LEON. Oh, is that what you think? Well, listen, Justine, in the past week, I have lost a wife and a publishing deal. A darts tournament is small potatoes, honey.

THE LOVE LIST

BILL. Wait a minute, Leon. I don't think you should take that tone with Justine.

LEON. You what?

BILL. I don't think you should talk to her that way.

LEON. Oh, is that so?

JUSTINE. All right, look you two. I don't want to be the cause of any friction here. Leon, you can talk to me any way you want. I'm a big girl and I can take as good as I can give. Bill, if you want me to move your material back out here, I will.

BILL. No, I don't want that, no.

JUSTINE. Are you sure?

BILL. I'm positive. Really.

JUSTINE. Well, would you at least go in and see how severely rearranged everything is?

BILL. Oh, I'm sure it's not bad at all.

JUSTINE. Well, just go and have a look. You've got me worried about it now.

BILL. All right, but I'm sure it's fine.

JUSTINE. Thank you, hon. Thank you.

(BILL EXITS to the hallway.)

LEON. All right, lady, listen here....

JUSTINE. No you listen, Leon. I know we don't see eye to eye on a lot of things, but I would like us to try and get along for Bill's sake. I think it hurts him when we argue.

LEON. Really?

JUSTINE. Yes. I mean his best friend and the woman he loves? When he sees us sniping at each other like this I'm sure it bothers him terribly.

LEON. His best friend and the woman he loves?

JUSTINE. Yes.

LEON. The woman he loves?

JUSTINE. Oh, all right, so you've known him longer than I have.

LEON. I should say I have.

JUSTINE. And you worked together at that newspaper all those years ago and you were there for him through his divorce from Roxanne and blah, blah, blah. I know all about that. But, let me tell you this, Leon. The love between a man and a woman is a very powerful force. And I don't think you want to make Bill choose between us. I don't think you want that. Because when it comes right down to it, I'm perfect for Bill in every way, and there's a lot more that I can do for him than any skirt chasing, past his prime, commercial fiction-writer can. Do you understand what I'm saying, Leon? Or am I being too erudite for a mainstream novelist such as yourself? No, you understand. I can see it in your face. You're always telling Bill that you're the only friend he's got. I think it just dawned on you that he's the only friend you've got too. So be nice to me, Leon. Be very nice. Or you'll be adding Bill to your recent spate of losses.

(BILL ENTERS from the hallway.)

BILL. Yeah I think I can have that straightened out in a week or two.

JUSTINE. Then it's not too bad?

BILL. No, it's nothing.

JUSTINE. Good. Well, I was just heading to bed. Are you coming in soon?

BILL. I'll be there in a couple of minutes.

JUSTINE. Okay. *(She gives BILL a kiss.)* Night Leon.

(JUSTINE EXITS to the hallway. LEON takes out the love list and a

pencil and begins erasing madly.)

BILL. What are you doing?

LEON. I've decided I'm not so fussy about a woman who speaks her mind. Now, what can I replace it with?

BILL. Tell me something. Have you ever heard of Willow Cosmetics?

LEON. Willow Cosmetics? No. Should I have?

BILL. Apparently they're the second largest cosmetics company in the country.

LEON. Sorry. Never heard of them. Oh, I know. When I was a child, my mother used to sing around the house all the time. I used to love that. *(He writes.)* Enjoys singing.

BILL. Are you really going to hand that in sometime?

LEON. As soon as I get it perfected. It's got to be just right. I don't want to wind up with someone like...uh....

(He stops short of saying JUSTINE.)

BILL. Andrea again?

LEON. Right. Andrea. Tell me something Billy. Friend to friend. Do you think I'm past my prime?

BILL. Past your prime? What, you mean as a writer?

LEON. As everything. Shit, all of a sudden I'm getting manuscripts turned down, my wife leaves me for someone else. I'm just starting to question my worth that's all. I mean, I'm a writer, but I'm not being published. That's like being a ball player and not making the team. I used to be a husband but now I'm not that anymore either.

BILL. Truth be told, Leon, you weren't much of a husband anyway.

LEON. Bugger off.

BILL. No, I don't think you're past your prime. Of course you're not. I mean, look at me. Fifty years old, no prospects, and Justine shows up.

LEON. Yes, that's a beacon of hope for the rest of us all right.

BILL. Take that list in. That'll cheer you up.

LEON. I will. I just have to do some more tweaking on it yet.

BILL. I like the singing idea. That's charming.

LEON. Goodnight, Bill.

BILL. Night, Leon.

(LEON EXITS. Off we hear JUSTINE singing. BILL turns the lights off and EXITS down the hallway. Lights down.)

Scene 2

(Time: Two days later. Place: The same. As the scene opens there is no one onstage. We hear JUSTINE singing offstage. [A different song this time.] The phone rings. BILL ENTERS from the hallway looking exhausted and fed up with the singing. He answers the phone.)

BILL. Hello?.....Hi, Leon........What?....I'm sorry, I can't hear you. Hang on a second... *(Calling offstage.)* Justine?!!! Can you stop singing for a moment please? I'm on the phone.

JUSTINE. *(Off.)* Sorry.

BILL. Yeah, hello, Leon.....Uh, sure, I guess I can go for breakfast this morning. Can you sing by and pick me up?...I mean, swing by and pick me up....She'll be leaving for work in two minutes?

THE LOVE LIST

Why?......All right, I'll see you in three minutes.

(He hangs up. JUSTINE ENTERS from the hallway, singing. She is getting ready for work.)

BILL. Justine? Justine? *(JUSTINE stops singing.)* Can we take a break from the singing for a while? Please?

JUSTINE. Oh. I didn't even realize I was doing it.

BILL. Sweetheart, you've been doing it steadily for the past two days.

JUSTINE. Have I really?

BILL. Yes.

JUSTINE. Well, I guess I'm just in a good mood. Who was on the phone?

BILL. Leon. He's coming to pick me up for breakfast.

(BILL goes to the refrigerator and takes out a paper bag.)

JUSTINE. That's nice. You two should spend more time to-gether.

BILL. Really?

JUSTINE. Yes. I like Leon. I think you two are good for each other.

(JUSTINE starts to sing again, a different song again, but BILL stops her.)

BILL. Justine? Justine? Look what I've got.

JUSTINE. What is it?

BILL. It's your lunch. I got up early and made it for you.

JUSTINE. You got up early just to make me lunch?

BILL. Actually your singing woke me up. So, I figured I'd put the time to good use.

JUSTINE. You are so sweet. Thank you, honey. *(She gives BILL a kiss and takes the bag. She sets it down on the counter as she continues to get organized.)* So, what are your plans for the day? After your breakfast I mean.

BILL. Well, I think I'll begin reorganizing my research material first.

JUSTINE. Bill, I'm really sorry about that.

BILL. Don't give it another thought. So, I'll work on that for a while and then I have to finish that housing report.

JUSTINE. Well, I'm not looking forward to my day. I've got a meeting with Mr. Jacobs and Brian Mercer at nine-thirty.

BILL. You didn't tell me that.

JUSTINE. I've been trying to put it out of my mind.

BILL. What's it about?

JUSTINE. Well, I think that after seeing Brian's Willow Cosmetics campaign, Mr. Jacobs wants to give the account back to me.

BILL. Well, that's good, isn't it? Wouldn't that be good?

JUSTINE. Yes, but just being in the same room with that muscle bound creep Brian Mercer makes my blood boil.

BILL. Tell me something. Where is this Willow Cosmetics located?

JUSTINE. Downtown.

BILL. I can't believe I've never heard of them.

JUSTINE. Yeah. Strange. Anyway, say hi to Leon for me.

BILL. I will. So, when will I see you again?

JUSTINE. I'll go to my place after work and get a change of clothes and I'll come over here around suppertime.

BILL. Tonight?

JUSTINE. Yes. Why? Don't you want me to?

BILL. Oh, yes. You know I want you to. I just wasn't sure if you wanted to.

THE LOVE LIST

JUSTINE. Why wouldn't I? I've been doing it every night for this long. Why would I stop now?

BILL. Well, I was afraid you might be getting bored with me. I mean you know what they say about us statisticians. We're as exciting as an Amish keg party.

JUSTINE. *(Stares at BILL.)* I don't get it.

BILL. Amish. Keg party. They don't drink.

JUSTINE. Sorry. Nothing. Well, gotta go. Bye-bye.

(She gives BILL a quick kiss and moves towards the door.)

BILL. Give em' hell today.

JUSTINE. Love you.

BILL. What?

JUSTINE. I said I love you.

BILL. Oh.

JUSTINE. What's wrong?

BILL. Nothing. I just...nothing.

JUSTINE. Okay. Bye-bye.

BILL. I love you too.

JUSTINE. I know you do.

(JUSTINE EXITS and closes the door. BILL notices the paper bag on the counter. He picks it up and rushes to the door.)

BILL. Justine! You forgot your lunch! *(BILL opens the door and looks out. JUSTINE is gone.)* Justine? Where the hell did she go? *(He closes the door.)* That's impossible. *(The door opens and JUSTINE ENTERS, startling BILL.)* Ah!!

JUSTINE. I forgot my lunch. *(She takes the bag from BILL.)* Thanks, sweetie.

(She turns for the door.)

BILL. Where were you?

JUSTINE. What?

BILL. Just now. Where did you go?

JUSTINE. What do you mean where did I go? I went out, and then I remembered my lunch and I came back.

BILL. But, I went....with the bag....and you were...

JUSTINE. Bill, I have to go. I'm going to be late. Bye, hon.

(JUSTINE EXITS and closes the door.)

BILL. But, Justine...

(BILL rushes to the door and opens it. JUSTINE is gone. He closes the door again.)

BILL. *(To himself.)* She's gone. What the hell is going on here? *(The door opens and JUSTINE ENTERS. BILL is startled.)* Ah!!

JUSTINE. I need a kiss for luck. (She kisses BILL.) Oh, I love kissing you. Bye-bye.

(JUSTINE EXITS and closes the door. There is a knock on the door.)

BILL. Ah!! Cut that out!!

(BILL opens the door. LEON is there.)

BILL. Leon?

(BILL pulls LEON inside, then looks into the hall.)

THE LOVE LIST

LEON. What are you doing?

BILL. Leon, you're not going to believe this. (He closes the door.)

LEON. What? . *(Beat as BILL hesitates.)* Bill, what is it?

BILL. A minute ago, Justine left for work, but she forgot her lunch so I ran out to get her and she wasn't there, and then I closed the door and all of a sudden it opened again and she was here, and then she left again and I ran out and she wasn't there, and then she came back for a kiss and she was here and then she left and you were there.

LEON. Jesus, Bill, I haven't even had a coffee yet.

BILL. Oh my God. No. This is crazy. This can't be.

LEON. What can't be?

BILL. Willow Cosmetics. Willow Cosmetics.

(He picks up a phone book and checks the yellow pages.)

LEON. Bill, what's going on?

BILL. I'm looking for Willow Cosmetics. She said they were downtown.

LEON. What's the matter? You out of blush?

BILL. Leon, two seconds before you knocked on my door, Justine walked out of that same door.

LEON. So?

BILL. So, did you see her out there?

LEON. No.

BILL. Exactly. So, where did she go?

LEON. I don't know. Maybe we just missed each other.

BILL. No. There's no way you could have missed her. *(Running his finger down the page.)* Willow. Willow. Ah-hah! No Willow Cosmetics. You see that? She said they were downtown and they're not in the phone book.

LEON. Maybe they're unlisted.

BILL. A business with an unlisted phone number?

LEON. Who cares about Willow Cosmetics? What's the problem?

BILL. What do you know about this Got A Match place?

LEON. What, the date finding service?

BILL. Yes.

LEON. Not much. She's been open for about two months and she runs the operation by herself.

BILL. This Gypsy woman?

LEON. Right. Why?

BILL. Look, Leon, either I'm having a nervous breakdown here or...No, it can't be. It's impossible.

LEON. What's impossible? What?

BILL. Well, this is going to sound completely insane, but...Oh, God...Leon, I don't think Justine exists outside of this apartment. Outside of my world.

LEON. Excuse me?

BILL. I don't think she exists.

LEON. I don't follow. What do you mean she doesn't exist?

BILL. Well—and I know this is totally nuts. It's preposterous—but, I think we might have created her.

LEON. What?

BILL With that list. She has all of the qualities that we put down on that list.

LEON. What are you talking about?

BILL. It's the only answer. We created her.

LEON. Bill, listen to yourself. Do you hear what you're saying? You're saying that because we wrote down some character traits on a list, that we created this woman?

BILL. I think we did, yes.

LEON. And when she leaves your world?

THE LOVE LIST

BILL. Pffftttt!!!

LEON. That's ridiculous.

BILL. It's the only possible explanation. That's why she knows so much about my work, about your infidelity, about everything. Somehow we conjured up this woman.

LEON. Oh, Bill, come on.

BILL. Well, look at her qualities. She likes kissing me, she leaves me alone when I ask her to, she's well-versed, she has a sense of humour, she...

LEON. Okay, you can stop right there because that's where your idea doesn't wash.

BILL. Why?

LEON. I changed the sense of humour this morning.

BILL. You what?

LEON. *(He takes out the list.)* I was going over the list and I thought of something else that would be much better.

BILL. And what's that?

LEON. She likes my friends and encourages me to spend time with them.

BILL. Oh my God!

LEON. What?

BILL. This morning she said she liked you. And she said you and I should spend more time together.

LEON. Justine said that?

BILL. Yes. And she's been singing ever since you put singing on the list.

LEON. Justine said she liked me?

BILL. Yes.

LEON. Then something is horribly awry.

BILL. Yes it is!! We created her!

LEON. You mean to tell me that every time we change something on the list, Justine changes too?

BILL. Yes. We regulate her personality!

(JUSTINE ENTERS through the front door. She startles BILL and LEON.)

JUSTINE. Crap!!
BILL.
LEON. tog. Ah!!!
JUSTINE. I am never going to get to work. Hi Leon.
LEON. Hello.
JUSTINE. *(To Bill.)* Can you believe it? I left my day planner on the night table. ·

BILL. Well, you know, Justine, that's better than leaving your night planner on the day table.

(He gives a little laugh.)

JUSTINE. I don't get it.
BILL. It's nothing. I'm sorry. Go ahead and get your day planner. *(JUSTINE EXITS to the hallway.)* See? No sense of humour.
LEON. That wasn't exactly a knee slapper, Bill. I need a pencil.

(He spots a pencil on the desk, picks it up and writes on the list.)

BILL. What are you doing?
LEON. I'm testing your theory.
BILL. What? Testing it how? What are you writing there?
LEON. Hold on.
BILL. Leon, you'd better not be writing 'large breasts'.

(LEON stops writing and erases what he has written. Then he writes something else.)

THE LOVE LIST

LEON. All right, there. *(LEON hands the list to BILL.)* Number eight.

BILL. *(Reading.)* Insecure? Why would you want her to be insecure?

LEON. Because you wouldn't let me write down large breasts.

(JUSTINE ENTERS.)

JUSTINE. All right. I think I'm finally set. God, I have never had so many false starts to a day. It's been one thing after another. *(The two men just stare at her.)* What's wrong?

BILL. Nothing.

JUSTINE. Why are you staring at me?

BILL. How are you feeling?

JUSTINE. I'm feeling fine.

BILL. Oh. Good.

JUSTINE. And you?

BILL. Fine.

JUSTINE. Good. Leon?

LEON. I'm good.

JUSTINE. Terrific. We're all good. I can go now. Bye-bye.

(JUSTINE EXITS out the door.)

LEON. You see? No change.

(JUSTINE ENTERS again.)

JUSTINE. Okay, what is it? Is it this outfit? Is that what you were staring at? Is there something wrong with it?

BILL. What? No. Your outfit's fine.

JUSTINE. Fine?

BILL. Yes. Fine.

JUSTINE. Fine how? Fine for a business meeting or fine for a rodeo? Explain fine.

BILL. Justine, you look great in that outfit. Really.

JUSTINE. Then it's my make-up, isn't it? You were staring at my make-up.

BILL. No, your make-up is fine too.

JUSTINE. Are you sure?

BILL. Positive:

JUSTINE. Because I'm going after the Willow Cosmetics account today and if my make-up isn't right then that could blow the whole thing for me.

BILL. No, it looks good.

JUSTINE. You think so?

BILL. It looks great.

JUSTINE. Oh, what do you know? You're a man. Leon, what do you think?

LEON. What?

JUSTINE. My make-up. Is it all right or do I look like I just fell face first onto a circus clown?

LEON. It looks good to me.

JUSTINE. No. No, I'll bet it looks just awful. I'd better double check for myself. Oh God. Oh God.

(JUSTINE EXITS down the hallway.)

BILL. Satisfied?

LEON. Well, I'll be damned.

BILL. *(He picks up the pencil and writes on the list.)* I'm changing that back to 'ambitious'. Now, what else have you done here? Oh, right. The singing. Thanks a lot. Were you out of your mind?

THE LOVE LIST

LEON. You said it was charming.

BILL. On paper maybe! I'll put 'unpredictable' back in there.

LEON. This is extraordinary.

BILL. Oh, and 'sense of humour'. I've got to put that back.

LEON. No, that'll mean discarding 'she likes your friends.'

BILL. I told you, Leon, a sense of humour is very important to me.

LEON. Then take out something else.

BILL. Like what?

LEON. Let me see that. *(LEON grabs the list and looks at it.)* 'Well-versed'. Well-versed is frivolous.

BILL. No, that's one of my favourites. That one stays.

LEON. All right then, 'ambitious'. Take out 'ambitious'.

BILL. You think so?

LEON. Yes, she already has a good job. You don't need that one. It's redundant.

BILL. All right. I'll replace 'ambitious' with 'sense of humour'.

(BILL takes the list and writes.)

LEON. *(Looking towards the hallway.)* Remarkable.

BILL. *(Has finished writing.)* There. Now this time, after she leaves, you open that door and you'll see.

LEON. See what?

BILL. Nothing. She'll be gone. She will have vanished into thin air.

LEON. All right look, Bill, I can buy the changing personality bit, but disappearing? I'm finding that hard to swallow.

(JUSTINE ENTERS from the hallway.)

JUSTINE. Finding what hard to swallow?

LEON. Hmm? Oh, I've..uh..I've got a lozenge stuck in my throat.

JUSTINE. You're just supposed to suck it, Leon. You're not supposed to swallow it.

LEON. I bow to your experience.

JUSTINE. Now that's funny. All right, this time I'm off for sure.

(She moves towards the door.)

BILL. Justine?

JUSTINE. Hmm?

BILL. Was your make-up all right after all?

JUSTINE. Are you kidding? I've never looked better. Have a nice breakfast, boys.

(JUSTINE EXITS out the door.)

BILL. Okay, now!

(LEON opens the door and looks out.)

LEON. She's gone.

BILL. I know she's gone!

LEON. That's incredible.

BILL. It's unbelievable.

LEON. Absolutely incredible.

(LEON closes the door.)

BILL. I told you.

LEON. My God. So, we invented this woman?

BILL. Invented her completely.

THE LOVE LIST

LEON. Mother of God. So, what do we do now?

BILL. There's only one thing we can do.

LEON. What's that?

BILL. We go with it.

LEON. We what? We go with it?

BILL. We go with it.

LEON. What do you think this is, like getting on the wrong bus? We can't just go with it. We've created somebody here, Bill. A person. That's a huge responsibility. No, I don't like this one bit.

BILL. Don't like it? It was your idea in the first place.

LEON. Oh, no. No, I just wanted to find you a woman. I did not want to create one. Creation is a little out of our league don't you think?

BILL. Well, I think she turned out all right for our first try.

LEON. Maybe she turned out too good.

BILL. Too good? How can she be too good?

LEON. Think about it. We only wrote down the ten qualities you wanted in a woman. There was nothing negative on that list.

BILL. Well, that's good.

LEON. No, it's not. You can't have a person who has no bad in them.

BILL. Why not?

LEON. Because it's not real. There is good and bad in every-one. That's what makes us human. That's what defines us. And keeping them properly balanced, that's our struggle. If we don't have that struggle, we have no purpose. Justine has no purpose. Her only reason for being here is to please you.

BILL. ......I'm supposed to say that's bad, aren't I?

LEON. It is bad.

BILL. Bad how?

LEON. It's too easy. There are no negatives to the relationship.

BILL. Bad how?

THE LOVE LIST

LEON. You need some bumps, Bill. Those conundrums, those problems that you have to work out together. That's the give and take. That's the cement in the relationship. With Justine, all you're going to be doing is taking.

BILL. I don't mind taking.

LEON. But, you're not giving.

BILL. Sure I'm giving.

LEON. Giving what? What are you giving?

BILL. A variety of things.

LEON. Like what?

BILL. I made her a lunch this morning. That's giving.

LEON. Oh, a lunch is giving.

BILL. It is. And I make love to her. That's giving.

LEON. No, that's taking.

BILL. No, it's giving.

LEON. No, no. Believe me, Billy. Where sex is concerned, the woman is giving, the man is taking. Make no mistake about that.

BILL. Well, maybe that's the way it is when you make love, but not when I do it. When I do it I try and make sure the woman is getting as much pleasure out of it as I am. I try and take my time with her. I search out the points on her body that are most sensitive.

LEON. Okay, first of all, don't ever describe your lovemaking techniques to me again. Now I'm going to have to go home, remove my brain, and boil it to get that image out of there. Secondly, even if the woman does get as much pleasure from it as we do, she is still the one who is giving, and we men should never forget that. In fact, we should fall on our knees and kiss their feet for being so generous.

BILL. I think you are jealous, Leon.

LEON. I am not jealous, damn it.

BILL. No, I think you are. You're jealous because I've got the perfect woman and you've got nobody. All right, look, why don't you go and get another blank love list from your Gypsy friend. My treat.

LEON. Oh what, you think this happens every time someone fills out one of those forms? Do you think these women are rolling off an assembly line like Chevrolets?! No! This is a fluke. There's a tear in the cosmic pie crust and you and I have somehow reached in and pulled out a plum. It's not right.

BILL. No. There's nothing wrong with it. It's perfect.

LEON. Perfect?

BILL. Yes, perfect. She's perfect.

LEON. No, no. Jesus, Bill. There's no such thing as perfection. You don't fall in love with a perfect person. You fall in love by learning to see an imperfect person perfectly.

BILL. Where did you hear that?

LEON. Shit, I think maybe I wrote it. Yes, I did, in Beyond Twilight. Pedantic my ass!

BILL. Well, I don't buy it.

LEON. Why not?

BILL. Well, because I think I'm...

LEON. You think you're what? I hope you're not going to say what I think you're going to say.

BILL. I think I'm...

LEON. No, don't say it, Bill..

BILL. I'm in love with her.

LEON. Oh, no!

BILL. Well, I think I am.

LEON. You can't be in love with her, Bill. She's not real.

BILL. Then that's her imperfection! And I'm falling in love with her by seeing that imperfection perfectly.

LEON. That's rubbish.

BILL. You wrote it.

LEON. I'm shallow!!

BILL. Leon, I'm in love with her. I am flat out, seat of my pants, head over heels in love with her.

LEON. Oh God, please, whatever you do, don't tell her that, because once you tell a woman that, there is no going back. It's like jumping off a cliff. And with the same results. You told her didn't you?

BILL. Yes.

LEON. Oh, Bill.

BILL. Damn it, Leon, you should be happy for me.

LEON. Happy for you? This is going to destroy you. How can I be happy about that?

BILL. It's not going to destroy me.

LEON. It most certainly is. I mean, if this woman is as perfect as you say she is, then how can she not demand perfection in return? How can she settle for a mate who is not her equal? And if, as I say, she is not perfect, then she will never live up to your expectations. You cannot win here.

BILL. I think maybe you should leave now.

LEON. What?

BILL. If you can't accept the woman I've chosen to be with then maybe you should leave.

LEON. The woman you've chosen to be with?

BILL. That's right, so would you go please?

LEON. Oh, so what am I, like her now? You ask me to leave and pfffft! Off I go? And when should I return, Master?

BILL. Maybe you shouldn't return at all.

(BILL moves to his desk and begins straightening up.)

LEON. What's that supposed to mean?

BILL. If you feel the way you feel, maybe you shouldn't come back.

LEON. What? Are you going to let this woman destroy our friendship?..... *(BILL doesn't answer.)* Bill, are you going to let this woman destroy our friendship?..... *(BILL doesn't answer.)* All right then, maybe I won't come back. Is that what you want? *(BILL doesn't answer.)* Fine. But, remember what I said. Perfection demands perfection.

(LEON turns to leave.)

BILL. Leon? That globalization book that Peter borrowed. I need it back.

(LEON EXITS. Lights down.)

Scene 3

(Time: That afternoon. Place: The same. As the lights come up there is no one onstage. JUSTINE ENTERS through the front door with her briefcase.)

JUSTINE. Bill? Are you home?

(BILL ENTERS from the hallway.)

BILL. Justine. I thought you weren't coming over until suppertime.
JUSTINE. I quit my job.
BILL. What?

THE LOVE LIST

JUSTINE. I quit. I've had enough of their bullshit.

BILL. You quit your job?

JUSTINE. I had to. If I stayed I wouldn't respect myself. I mean, at the meeting this morning, Mr. Jacobs handed me a new client list and it showed that he'd given my two biggest accounts to Brian Mercer. It was an enormous slap in the face.

(She moves to the kitchen area and pours herself a drink.)

BILL. You quit your job?

JUSTINE. And the whole time that pretty boy Brian just sat there in his fancy Armani suit wearing that smug little smirk of his. I would have kicked him in the balls if I thought he had any. So, I told Mr. Jacobs that he was making a big mistake and that I wasn't going to sit still for it. Then I tore up the client list and threw it across the table at him. And then Brian says, 'Well, aren't you the little tiger.' What a prick. I showed him though. I picked up the pitcher of water that was sitting there and I hit him in the face with it.

BILL. You threw water in his face?

JUSTINE. No, I hit him with the pitcher. I think I might've broken his nose. I'm not sure. And then I went downstairs and I slashed the tires on his Corvette.

BILL. You what?

JUSTINE. Well, I didn't do it. I paid a street person to do it.

BILL. A street person?

JUSTINE. Well, she was right there and she looked like she could use the money.

BILL. Oh, my God.

JUSTINE. I will not stand for being treated like that. Being spoken to in that manner. He's just lucky I didn't do more.

BILL. More? You broke his nose and slashed his tires. That's more than the Godfather would have done.

JUSTINE. What was that? Was that supposed to be funny?

BILL. Well...

JUSTINE. Because I'm not in a laughing mood right now, Bill.

BILL. Really? I thought I put 'sense of humour' back in.

JUSTINE. You what?

BILL. Hang on a second. *(He moves to his desk drawer, takes out the list and looks at it.)* Yes, there it is. Number eight.

(He puts the list back and closes the desk drawer again.)

JUSTINE. What in the hell are you talking about?!

BILL. It's hard to explain.

JUSTINE. Never mind. I'm sorry. I don't know why I'm snapping at you. I guess you just happen to be in the wrong place at the wrong time.

BILL. Well, it is my place.

JUSTINE. That's another thing.

BILL. What is?

JUSTINE. Well, me being out of a job, I don't know if I can afford that expensive apartment anymore. It looks like I'm going to have to move now.

BILL. Don't worry, you'll find another job.

JUSTINE. I don't want another job.

BILL. Of course you do.

JUSTINE. No, I'm sick of work. In fact, I think I could be quite content just sitting at home all day. I could watch television, read People Magazine, play the lottery.

BILL. *(To himself.)* Damn. No ambition.

JUSTINE. What?

BILL. Uh...I was just saying that if you can do that°Xyou know, afford not to work°Xthen that's great. I mean, if you've got a nest egg stashed away to carry you through. Do you have a nest egg?

JUSTINE. Oh, God, no. I haven't got a pot to piss in. But, I was thinking that if it's all right with you, maybe I could move in here.

BILL. Move in here? With me?

JUSTINE. Yeah.

BILL. You want to piss in my pot?

JUSTINE. Well, I'm over here all the time anyway, so why not just move in? Oh, it would be wonderful, Bill. You would be working in the spare room and I'd be out here doing nothing.

BILL. The spare room?

JUSTINE. Well, it makes sense. I mean your research material is in there.

BILL. Uh-huh.

JUSTINE. Speaking of which, did you get it all straightened out?

BILL. Uh..I've put quite a dent in it.

JUSTINE. Well go ahead and work on it. I don't want to keep you from it.

BILL. No, it can wait.

JUSTINE. Bill, please. Go. I know how important it is to you. Besides, I'm not very good company right now.

BILL. Well, I think we should talk.

JUSTINE. Oh, I couldn't now. Besides, I'll feel so much better when your research is put back the way it was.

BILL. Well, all right. But, you know we really should talk about this moving in idea before the day's out.

JUSTINE. We will.

BILL. Promise?

JUSTINE. Definitely. But, right now I just want to relax for a bit. Gather my thoughts.

BILL. All right. I'll be in the...spare room if you need me.

THE LOVE LIST

(BILL EXITS to the hallway. The phone rings.)

JUSTINE. I'll get it. *(She answers the phone.)* Hello?.....Yes, he is. May I ask who's calling?.......Rachel?.... And what is this regarding Rachel?......Why not? Is it personal?.......It is? Well, that's all I wanted to know. That's all you had to say. Now, that wasn't so difficult, was it, Rachel? The next time someone asks you what a phone call is regarding, you might try and be a little more forthcoming instead of wasting people's time.

(JUSTINE hangs up the phone. BILL ENTERS.)

BILL. Who was it?

JUSTINE. Who the hell is Rachel?

BILL. Rachel?

JUSTINE. Yes, Rachel.

BILL. Oh, Rachel. She helped me with the housing survey last week. Yes. She's coming to town and she wants to do some follow-up work.

JUSTINE. Did you sleep with her?

BILL. What? No. Last week? No.

JUSTINE. Are you lying to me?

BILL. No. We just made plans to get together this week over dinner.

JUSTINE. Over dinner?

BILL. Yes.

JUSTINE. You mean a date?

Bil: No, not a date. She's from out of town and she doesn't know where the restaurants are so I offered to take her to one.

JUSTINE. Is she stupid?

BILL. What?

JUSTINE. I said is she stupid? If you don't take her to a restaurant will she just sit in her room and starve to death?

BILL. Wait a minute. Don't you trust me? Because you're supposed to trust me.

JUSTINE. Should I trust you, Bill? Can I trust you?

BILL. That's not the point. The point is you're supposed to.

JUSTINE. Who said?

BILL. Well, it was on the uh...

JUSTINE. It was on the what?

BILL. You know what this is? I'll bet this is all because of that 'unpredictable' that I put back in. Leon warned me about that.

JUSTINE. Are you sleeping with this woman or not?

BILL. No, I'm not.

JUSTINE. Because don't expect me to move in here and try and make a life for the two of us if you're going to act like your sleazy friend Leon. I will not put up with that kind of behavior.

BILL. You don't like Leon now?

JUSTINE. I've never liked Leon, you know that. Oh, God, now I'm getting a headache. I think I'll take a couple of aspirins and lie down. Maybe I'll read for a bit.

BILL. Good idea. Read yourself to sleep. Let your cares float away on the wings of Tennyson.

JUSTINE. You know, Bill, if I do move in we're going to have to re-decorate.

BILL. What?

JUSTINE. And I mean a complete overhaul. And that includes you.

BILL. Me?

JUSTINE. Yes. You're a fashion catastrophe. But, don't worry. I'll have you looking stylish yet.

BILL. I pray that you can. *(JUSTINE EXITS to the hallway. To JUSTINE.)* Sweet dreams! *(To himself.)* Sweet Jesus! That 'unpredictable' is overriding everything. *(There is a knock on the door.)*

Oh, now what?

(BILL opens the door. LEON is there with a book.)

BILL. Leon!
LEON. Here's your book, asshole.
BILL. Come in, quickly!

(BILL pulls LEON into the room.)

LEON. What's the matter?
BILL. Oh, it's a mess. It's a complete mess.
LEON. What is?
BILL. Justine. She quit her job, she doesn't trust me anymore, she's trying to change me, and now she wants to move in with me.
LEON. My God, maybe she's real after all.
BILL. No, no! It's like Westworld and she's Yul Brynner. She's running amok. I don't know what she's going to do next.

(BILL goes to the drawer and takes out the list.)

LEON. Well, you wanted unpredictable.
BILL. I know. I know. I'm going to take that out and put something else in there. I just need you to help me think of what.
LEON. Oh, no.
BILL. What's the matter?
LEON. So, every time she does something that you don't approve of you're going to change her?
BILL. No, just this one last change and I think I'll have it where I want it. I mean, right now it's totally out of whack.

(JUSTINE ENTERS from the hallway.)

JUSTINE. Bill, I can't find the aspirin. Oh, hi Leon.

LEON. Hello.

JUSTINE. What brings you here?

LEON. I'm returning a book.

JUSTINE. Oh. You read?

BILL. The aspirin is on the bookcase in the bedroom, Justine.

JUSTINE. Thank you. Leon.

LEON. Cruella.

(JUSTINE EXITS to the hallway.)

BILL. Please, Leon help me out. What can I put down in place of unpredictable?

LEON. Bill, I don't want any part of this.

BILL. How about sensitive? Caring. I mean right now she's a little harsh, so I think if we turn down the harshness and turn up the sensitivity we might be on to something. Yeah, that's what we'll do. *(He writes.)* Sensitive. Feeling.

LEON. Bill, this is not right. You're acting like Dr. Frankenstein here.

BILL. No. Look. I'm done. That's it. The list is complete now. All finished. *(JUSTINE ENTERS from the hallway. She is crying.)* Justine? What's wrong?

JUSTINE. Leon, I'm sorry.

LEON. What?

JUSTINE. I'm sorry I made fun of your reading skills a moment ago. And I'm sorry I said I didn't like your book.

LEON. Oh, you like it now?

JUSTINE. No, I'm just sorry I said I didn't. Can you ever forgive me?

LEON. Uh.. sure, Justine. Sure.

THE LOVE LIST

JUSTINE. Oh, thank you. And Bill, I'm sorry I hung up on your tramp.

BILL. No, she's not a tramp, Justine.

JUSTINE. Yes, she is. I'm sorry. *(She hugs BILL.)* I am so sorry.

LEON. What tramp?

BILL. Rachel from last week.

LEON. She's a tramp?

Bil: No, she's..can this wait?!!

JUSTINE. I should phone that son of a bitch Brian Mercer and tell him I'm sorry I broke his nose.

BILL. Justine, you know what I think? I think you should go back in and lie down.

JUSTINE. You do?

BILL. Oh, absolutely.

JUSTINE. Why?

BILL. Well, Leon and I are discussing a matter of great importance here, so...

JUSTINE. Oh, I'm sorry. Did I interrupt? Oh, God, I'm sorry. What was I thinking? I am so thoughtless. My mother used to tell me that all the time. And sometimes she'd become so agitated that her cigarette would pop out of her mouth and roll down the front of her sundress and she'd start slapping herself. *(She begins slapping herself on the torso.)* Oh, God, I miss that woman so much.

(JUSTINE EXITS to the hallway crying.)

BILL. All right, sensitive goes.

(He erases sensitive.)

LEON. I thought you said you were finished changing her.

BILL. Well, I can't leave her like that!

LEON. Bill, don't do this.

BILL. Just this one more. This will be it for sure.

LEON. You said the last one was it.

BILL. I know.

LEON. You said you were done.

BILL. Well, I'm not done!! Goddamn it, Leon, I am this close to having the perfect woman!! Do you understand what that means? Perfection. A statistician's dream. No runs, no hits, no errors. One hundred percent of the sample returned. Now, please, help me out here. Please?

LEON. ....All right, but this is the last one.

BILL. Definitely. Thank you.

LEON. And I'm only doing this because I feel responsible for getting you this gift in the first place.

BILL. Fine. Now, let's think. What can we put down in place of sensitive?

LEON. Well, whatever it is just make sure it can't backfire on you. Something harmless like 'good speller'.

BILL. Oh right. Just what I need. Someone correcting my spelling twenty-four hours a day. That's worse than your singing idea. No. No, I've got it. Fun-loving.

(He writes on the list.)

LEON. Fun-loving?

BILL. Yeah, I mean, what can be more harmless than fun-loving?

LEON. That's what you thought about sensitive.

BILL. No, this is good. She'll probably enjoy a sprightly game of Scrabble or watching a good documentary on television.

LEON. You and I certainly have different ideas of what fun is.

(JUSTINE ENTERS from the hallway.)

JUSTINE. Bill, let's go out.

BILL. What?

JUSTINE. Let's go out. I feel like doing something.

BILL. But, I thought you were tired.

JUSTINE. No, I've got my second wind and I'm ready to rock! Let's go dancing!

BILL. What? Dancing? No! I'm a terrible dancer.

JUSTINE. Oh, come on! Let's throw caution to the wind.

(JUSTINE turns the CD player on. We hear an up tempo song. JUSTINE begins to dance. BILL turns off the music.)

BILL. No, I never throw caution to the wind unless I'm teth-ered.

JUSTINE. Well, let's do something. Let's find an amusement park and ride the roller coaster.

BILL. Roller coaster?

JUSTINE.Yes.'God. Anything.

LEON. Perhaps there's a riveting documentary on television.

JUSTINE. No, I want some excitement. Like rock climbing, or surfing, or hang gliding! There's an idea.

BILL. Hang gliding??

JUSTINE. Yeah!

BILL. No, I'm not good with heights, Justine.

JUSTINE. Oh, don't be a stick in the mud. You're going and you'll love it. Now, we'll have to pack a lunch. Let's see what we've got here. *(JUSTINE goes to the refrigerator, bends over and looks in. BILL erases something on the list and writes something else down.)* Maybe I could whip up a salad of some kind. *(JUSTINE suddenly stands up. She speaks with a southern accent now.)* Oh, dear.

    BILL. Justine?

    JUSTINE. Oh, dear.

(She fastens a button on her blouse.)

    BILL. What's wrong?

    JUSTINE. What's wrong? My blouse was undone. My womanhood was exposed for all the world to see.

    LEON. It was just the top button.

    JUSTINE. You were looking??

    LEON. What??

    JUSTINE. You were looking down my blouse? *(To Bill.)* Leon was looking down my blouse.

    BILL. No he wasn't. Don't be silly.

    JUSTINE. I am so embarrassed.

    LEON. It was one button, Justine. I couldn't see anything.

    JUSTINE. *(To Bill.)* You see? He was looking.

    BILL. No, of course he wasn't looking. Were you, Leon?

    LEON. Of course I was.

    BILL. What?

    LEON. She's a beautiful woman. Of course I was looking.

    JUSTINE. *(To Leon.)* I'm what? I'm beautiful?

    LEON. Yes, you are.

    JUSTINE. Oh, I am not. I declare. I'm average-looking at best.

    LEON. Justine, you're being too modest. Way too modest. Bill, don't you think Justine is too modest?

    BILL. No, I like this. It's very coquettish.

    JUSTINE. That reminds me, I have to go out today and buy some flannel pajamas.

    BILL. What?

    JUSTINE. Yes, I can't believe I have been sleeping in the nude with you. A woman should be more reserved where her body is concerned.

BILL. Flannel pajamas?

JUSTINE. And the thicker the better. *(BILL motions for Leon to go to the list. LEON goes to the list and erases something. He frantically writes down something else.)* And I should get some more sensible underwear as well. This Victoria's Secret line I've been wearing is so impractical.

BILL. Hurry, Leon!

JUSTINE. In fact, I do believe I'll go shopping right now. This very minute. Now, where did I leave my car keys?

(JUSTINE moves to BILL's desk to look for her keys.)

LEON. Done!

(JUSTINE stares at the work on the desk. She no longer speaks with a southern accent.)

JUSTINE. Bill?

BILL. Yes?

JUSTINE. In this housing report?

BILL. Yes?

JUSTINE. Deterrence is misspelled.

BILL. It is?

JUSTINE. Of course it is. Deterrence. D-e-t-e-r-r-e-n-c-e. Deterrence.

BILL. *(Looks to LEON.)* Well, thank you. I'll see that it's corrected.

(BILL tries to take the list from LEON. A struggle ensues that JUSTINE does not notice. She continues to speak.)

THE LOVE LIST

JUSTINE. I certainly hope so. Oh, and here's another one. Impetus. I-m-p-e-t-u-s. Impetus.

(During BILL and LEON's struggle, the list is ripped in half. JUSTINE stiffens. BILL and LEON look at JUSTINE.)

BILL. Justine? Are you all right?

JUSTINE. Uh....yes. Fine. I just lost my train of thought. Train of thought. Train of thought. What was I saying?

(BILL takes the other half of the list from LEON, goes to his desk and staples it together.)

LEON. Uh..spelling. You were noticing some spelling mistakes in Bill's work.

JUSTINE. Oh, right. God, look at all of this work. This is why we never go out, isn't it? Your work is taking up all of your time. *(JUSTINE notices BILL putting tape on the list now.)* Is that what this is? More work?

(JUSTINE grabs the love list from Bill.)

BILL. No, Justine, that's not work.

JUSTINE. *(Reading.)* The Love List. What's this?

BILL. It's nothing.

JUSTINE. *(Reading.)* Ten qualities I am looking for in a mate. What is this?

BILL. It's nothing. Really. Leon and I were just....

JUSTINE. Just what?

LEON. I was just making out a list of the ten things I look for in a woman. You know, because I'm single now and I thought I should just recap.

JUSTINE. *(To BILL.)* Ohhhh. This is that list you keep mentioning. *(Reading.)* Tidy, enjoys kissing...

BILL. Yeah, Justine you don't have to read that.

JUSTINE. No, this is interesting.

BILL. But it's Leon's personal list.

JUSTINE. Oh, Leon doesn't mind if I look, do you Leon?

LEON. Well, actually, it is kind of...

JUSTINE. Yes, this is very interesting. Hmm. You know what? I'm going to make out my own list.

(She picks up a pencil.)

BILL. You're what?

JUSTINE. I'm going to make out a list of the ten things I look for in a mate. Just to refresh myself, like Leon here.

LEON. No, you probably shouldn't do that, Justine.

JUSTINE. It'll just take a second. *(She begins erasing.)* Now we'll get rid of that, and that, and that..

BILL. Justine, please, don't...

JUSTINE. *(She stops erasing.)* Oh.

(We think she's been altered.)

BILL. Oh, no. What's wrong, Justine?

JUSTINE. *(Pointing to the list.)* .....Number four. Leon, you naughty boy. We'll keep that one. Oh what the hell, we'll get rid of everything else and start fresh.

BILL. Justine, no.

LEON. Oh, God.

JUSTINE. *(She erases and then she stops and closes her eyes.)* Oh, my. Oh my.

BILL. What is it?

JUSTINE. I don't know. I feel kind of unemcumbered all of a sudden. It just swept over me like a wave. Woo! Okay, number one.

BILL. Justine, please.

JUSTINE. Good looking.

BILL. I really wish you..Good looking?

JUSTINE. Yeah.

BILL. Good looking is number one??

JUSTINE. Sure. A man's looks are important to me.

LEON. Well, that's pretty damned shallow.

JUSTINE. Number two, physically fit. Number three, nice dresser...

BILL. Now wait a minute, wait.

JUSTINE. What's wrong?

BILL. These are all surface things. Superficial.

JUSTINE. Oh, I beg to differ. What I'm doing here is laying the foundation. You see, a man who possesses these attributes is also going to be self-assured, poised, and admired. He is going to have one foot in the door of success no matter what career path he chooses. And superficial or not, that's the way the world works. Now, may I continue?

BILL. Justine, I really don't think this is a good idea.

JUSTINE. Number four stays.. *(After a beat she writes.)* ...without having to ask for it. Number five, creative. Number six, can make love for long stretches at a time.

BILL. Oh, well now you're just being mean.

JUSTINE. Number seven, spontaneous. I love spontaneous men. Number eight, nice ass.

LEON.

BILL. tog. Nice ass?!

JUSTINE. Number nine, tall.

BILL. Tall? Tall?!

JUSTINE. And number ten, likes fast cars.

BILL. Oh, come on! Justine, that list is entirely unrealistic.

JUSTINE. Why?

BILL. Why? Because you've described a man who doesn't exist.

JUSTINE. Oh, I think there are plenty of men out there who meet these qualifications.

BILL. Oh, I doubt it, Justine. I doubt it very much.

LEON. Are you sure you're not just jealous of that fellow, Bill?

BILL. Jealous? No, I'm not jealous. I'm just being factual. After all, I am a man of statistics and I'm telling you right now, that the chances of that man existing are ten thousand to one.

(There is a loud knock on the door. BILL, LEON, and JUSTINE all look towards the door.)

JUSTINE. I'll get it.

BILL & LEON. *(Together.)* No!!

(Blackout. *The break between these two scenes must go quickly or the audience will think it is the end of the show.)

Scene 4
Epilogue

(Time: A few minutes later. Place: The same. The lights come up to reveal BILL and LEON seated on the couch.)

LEON. Well, you must admit, Billy, he had a nice ass.

BILL. Snappy dresser too.

LEON. And a good-looking fellow I think, although it was hard to tell with that cast on his nose.

BILL. I should have known she was attracted to him. He's all she ever talked about.

LEON. Ah, you had no way of knowing. You thought she hated him.

BILL. Yes, but what I mistook for hate was actually sexual tension. Damn, I shouldn't have let her go. I should have fought for her.

LEON. It would have been a terribly short fight.

BILL. I should have at least taken the list back from her. Stupid!

LEON. Bill, I think we're much better off without the list. Good Lord, can you imagine if that list had fallen into the hands of two less responsible men?

BILL. So, tell me this, if he came from the same place she came from...

LEON. Then that's where they exist now. Which means they don't exist.

BILL. And I'll never see her again.

LEON. Touch wood.

BILL. Damn it. I've waited so long to feel that way about someone. And then to finally have her and let her get away.

LEON. I know what you mean.

BILL. No, I don't think you do. Hell, women come and go in your world. They always have. But, me, what's the likelihood of a woman that's so right for me, coming along again in my lifetime? Do you know what the odds are? I'd put it at seven hundred and fifty to one. No, we only get so many chances in this life, Leon. We can't be driving on past them like they were meaningless signposts on the side of the road. I don't want my life to be a series of missed opportunities. God, maybe you weren't so wrong after all when you accepted those cake invitations. I mean, the door opened and you walked through it. You lived! You experienced life! What have I done? Discovered how many adults there are per household in the average single family dwelling. Two and a half, in case you're interested.

(The phone rings. BILL answers it.)

BILL. Hello?...... Speaking......Oh, hi Rachel...... Yes, I know you called. I heard.... Yes, I'm sorry about that....... Well, that was Justine..... No, no nothing like that. She was just a friend. But, she's gone now. Gone for good. *(He runs his finger over the desk.)* Uh-huh... Yes, I know she was rude to you on the phone, but.. well.. nobody's perfect. *(He rubs the dust off of his finger.)* Rachel, listen. I know you're in town on business, but I really think we hit it off last week and I'd like to take you out on an actual bona fide date........ That's right. We'll do anything you want to do. You just name it.......... Dancing? Of course we can go dancing. What the hell? Let's throw caution to the wind..... *(LEON gets up and moves to the door.)* Good. Where are you staying?...... All right, I'll pick you up there at eight. See you then.

(BILL hangs up the phone.)

Leon? Where are you going?

LEON. Well, I think I'm..... I'm going to go home, Bill. I'm going to go home and I'm going to phone Andrea and I'm going to tell her that I don't blame her for having an affair and I don't blame her for leaving me. I'm going to tell her that I have been an arrogant, self-centred, unadulterated ass throughout our entire twenty-four years together and if she lives to be a hundred, she should never have to put up with a disingenuous, pissant like me ever again.

BILL. Good for you, Leon.

LEON. But if there is a chance—any chance at all that she might still feel something for me—then I would be thrilled to have her come back. And I would do my damnedest to be the kind of husband that she deserves, because she is as perfect as they come, Billy, and it's about time I started treating her that way. *(He opens the door.)* And then I'm going to get my money back from that fucking Gypsy.

(LEON EXITS. Music up. Lights down. End.)

THE LOVE LIST

PROPERTIES

Many, many stacks of newspapers
Many, many magazines
Many, many file folders
Many, many books
Telephone
wine glasses
Whiskey glasses
Juice glasses
Large carving knife
Coffee maker
2 coffee mugs
Corkscrew
Wine bottle
Three different whiskey bottles
Love list in envelope
Laptop
Pencils with erasers
Orange juice
Newspaper for LEON
Grocery bag
Chicken breasts
Romaine lettuce
Portobello mushrooms
Strawberries
Briefcase for JUSTINE
Briefcase for BILL
Lunch bag
CD player and speakers
Globalization book
Book of poetry
Frying pan
Suitcase
Day planner
Phone book

THE LOVE LIST

COSTUMES

ACT I

Scene 1

BILL: slacks, shirt, pullover sweater, dress shoes, windbreaker
LEON: leather coat, dress shirt, dark slacks, dress shoes

Scene 2

BILL: slacks, shirt, pullover sweater, dress shoes
JUSTINE: business suit, heels, purse

Scene 3

BILL: suit, tie, dress shoes
LEON: leather coat, sweater, cords, dress shoes

Scene 4

BILL: suit, tie, dress shoes
LEON: sport coat, sweater, cords, dress shoes
JUSTINE: business suit, heels, purse

Scene 5

BILL: housecoat, t-shirt, boxer shorts, slippers, then changes into slacks and shirt
LEON: leather coat, t-shirt, cords, dress shoes
JUSTINE: nightgown, rubber gloves

THE LOVE LIST

ACT II

Scene 1

BILL: windbreaker, shirt, slacks, casual shoes
LEON: leather coat, t-shirt under a shirt, black jeans, casual shoes
JUSTINE: nightgown, rubber gloves

Scene 2

BILL: shirt, slacks, casual shoes
LEON: leather coat, t-shirt, black jeans, casual shoes
JUSTINE: business suit, heels, purse

Scene 3

BILL: shirt, slacks, casual shoes
LEON: leather coat, shirt, black jeans, casual shoes
JUSTINE: business suit, heels, purse

Scene 4

BILL: shirt, slacks, casual shoes
LEON: leather coat, shirt, black jeans, casual shoes

Late Flowering
JOHN CHAPMAN and IAN DAVIDSON

These masters of uproarious comedy have created another delightfully funny cast of characters. Constance Beauchamp, an elegant spinster, runs a marriage bureau for the well-to-do in a fashionable area of London. She is assisted by a hard-working secretary who is set in her ways and happy with her old-fashioned filing system. Constance insists on installing a computer. The man who comes to teach them how to use it is an odd-ball bachelor who decides to feed in his own profile through the machine to find an ideal mate. After some hilarious trials and errors, Constance is alarmed to discovers it's her! 1 m., 4 f. (#13834)

The Trouble with Trent
FRED CARMICHAEL

Sparkling dialogue and laughs galore abound in this tale of mistaken identities that begins when three mystery buffs who become acquainted on the Internet E-mail chapters to each other and meet for two weeks to polish off their first book. Book sales soar when their agent hints that Sarah Trent, the pen name they use, is a real person. Meanwhile, a Washington socialite being blackmailed intends to send Sarah a story she has written about herself. She mistakenly sends the manuscript to the blackmailer and the payoff money to the three ladies behind the name Trent who have gathered to write another book. Government agents pursuing the blackmailer and a man claiming to be Mr. Trent are just two of the people who pop up. This is first-rate comedy by the popular author of numerous widely produced plays. 2 m., 6 f. (#22744)

**Send for your copy of the Samuel French
BASIC CATALOGUE OF PLAYS AND MUSICALS**

CAPTIVATING PLAYS FOR SMALL CASTS

JERRY AND TOM
Rick Cleveland

A man who is tied to a chair with a bag over his head is telling jokes to Jerry and Tom while they wait for a phone call instructing them to kill him. In a series of similarly intense vignettes, a Chicago hit man plays mentor to his impatient cohort in this horrifyingly hysterical comedy. The film was selected for screening at the Sundance Film Festival. 3 m. Various sets (simply suggested). (#22194)

"Viciously funny." — *Los Angeles Times*

"Hilarious." — *Los Angeles Weekly*

"Terrifyingly funny little gem." — *Los Angeles Reader*

THE MOONS OF ALNYRON
Brandy Walker

In this mysterious and unpredictable play about space, a brilliant young scientist is confronted by his employer for falling behind in his work. Embarrassed and apologetic, he explains that he has become obsessed with his research on the planet Alnyron and its three moons. He is referred to an elderly, asthmatic psychiatrist and arrives at her office, to her horror, with countless boxes of papers and files documenting everything about Alnyron, from its unique geology to extraterrestrial poetry. He describes strange peoples and odd-colored sunsets and gives lectures on alien holidays and moon colonists. Undaunted, the doctor attempts to unravel his intricate, deep space world with startling results. 1 m., 1 f. *set Unit set. (#15171)